If I Should Die Before It Wakes

And Other Stories

By Allen Whitlock

All rights reserved.
Copyright © 2012 Allen Whitlock
Cover art Copyright © 2011 MaryAnn Puls
Jacket Design, MaryAnn Puls
Photo, Philippe Assaf, Philo Photography

ISBN 10: 1477557873
ISBN 13: 978-1477557877

For Judy

ACKNOWLEDEGEMENTS

Sincere thanks to everyone who helped with this body of work, may none of the faults or errors reflect upon them:

I heap much praise upon my fantastic and dedicated editor Andrew Steiner. Thank you MaryAnn Puls (sister) for the amazing cover art and jacket design. Thanks to Professors Rebeca Castellanos and Médar Serrata who prodded me to produce this collection in book form. And of course much gratitude goes to my lovely wife Judy for her love, patience, and encouragement and for her example of hard work and dedication to her teaching and writing. Thank you to Rob Alt, Kate McCrindle, Roger Gillis, Joe Abramajtys, and Bonnie Jo Campbell.

If I Should Die Before It Wakes

Table of Contents

Concerning the Death of Robert Logan on CV-IV 1
Assisted Living 17
I Follow the Sun 25
Killing Time 55
Out of Sight 85
If I Should Die Before It Wakes 101

Concerning the Death of Robert Logan on CV-IV

By the time we arrived at CV-IV, the lure of solid earth and a blue cloud-dotted sky had poisoned all reason. We were transfixed—gazing down at a planet with Earth-like gravity, a temperate climate, and large oceans. We detected no sentient life, but almost drooled on the magnified images on our screens; roadways broke the lush landscape into crescent sections with a strange, mathematical precision. How familiar and yet how alien was this metropolitan layout. Someone had to have built those cities, yet there was no life.

Those first ships were too cramped for our crew of twenty-four and a mission lasting three years. Homesickness may be purely psychological, but it hit us all in the gut with a physical force.

We were largely academics after all—a hasty stew of specialties thrust into roles for which none was truly prepared.

Sent simply to observe, we carried no armaments and no security personnel. It was assumed, perhaps correctly, that a bunch of academics might not react with due calm, and, if armed might react unwisely to unknown threats. For example, after having landed (perhaps after some seriously shoddy life-scan investigation, not to cast aspersions on the biologists) on the fourth planet of the Reticulous Prime solar system, we found ourselves swarmed by twelve foot long black and orange snake-like creatures with glowing eyes the size of chicken eggs. If we had weapons we would have caused an incident. The Reticulousians turned out to be a rather charming race with a complex language expressed in a highly coordinated *group dance*. In fact, in my spare time I am attempting to finish the translation of their great epic poem, *The Egg of Gyztoian*.

My specialty is xenolinguistics. That was also Robert's specialty. There were three xenolinguistics experts on our ship. Communications was considered key to our mission. Remember, this was a crew designed and outfitted, not by the experts but rather by nervous politicians and the government—need I say more?

The third linguist on the mission was Cerna Mures. Concerning Cerna, and I say this as a linguist, I could not often understand her. She was a thin-framed mousey thing, given to long bouts of staring into the distance. Silence is an odd trait for a linguist and that led to some of us suspected her of being a fraud. Nevertheless, I soon found that her reasoning was on some plane of intelligence far above my own. At times, on matters linguistical, I felt I might as well have been an amoeba talking to Einstein. I'd take her anti-social behavior as rude but considering the reverse, what fool would talk to an amoeba? I began to understand the reason for her silence.

When Cerna was not reading her screen or staring blankly at the wall, she was eating, a task preformed with the intensity of a starving dog.

If I ever became stuck on an interpretation, I could take it to her. She would stare and knit together her brows, consult a screen, and then write out a translation, an explanation, or make a simple drawing illustrating the idea, or merely point to the screen without speaking and raise her eyes to me with a curiously distressed expression as though to ask, *is that correct?* It was a strange dichotomy of intellectual superiority and social inferiority. Sometimes she would speak aloud, but usually only to ask you to pass some food at the table.

Robert, on the other hand, jabbered incessantly. There is no weather on a spacecraft, but that was the base stratum of his blatherings. One not only learned how well or how poorly Robert had slept the night before but one also received a careful comparison to his previous night's slumber. Any excuse to chatter was leapt upon and when there was no conversation, he prompted one with inane questions. *Does it seem cold in here to you? Does it seem warm in here?*

Even if you didn't respond, you were not immune because Robert could find a conversation-starter lurking in any nearby object, a salt shaker, a fork—he would look at his watch, and the simple clock face would inspire him to declare any number of things, *My dog is probably just getting up right now!* Or, *sunrise on my cabin on the lake about now… did I tell you about my house on the lake?* Chatter concerning the temporal was particularly annoying to the ship's engineer who soon grew tired of explaining the relative nature of time, falling in and out of synch with Earth time, as we stretched in and out of normal space, like a rubber band, always returning to its original shape.

Despite my annoyance, Robert entertained most of the people most of the time, and he took on something like a leadership position in most people's eyes. It was, ironically, his own charismatic nature that led to his doom.

Only a year and a half into the mission, we had some real hits under our belts, cracking languages. The first was the post-mineral society of Jat; our orbital interception of radio wave broadcasts worked perfectly. We linguists had a field day listening in at Tlön, whose inhabitants were somehow communicating without any part of speech we would call nouns. Even limited as we were to those planets where the population used radio and other electromagnetic communication, our cup overflowed.

We succeeded in collecting information for later study, with no contact, per what we laughingly refer to as *The Prime Directive*. We actually had no such paternalistic pseudo-ethic under the noble guise of non-interference, but rather it was that our betters decided that contact would be made... later, in a follow-up phase. Our imperative was that we could only listen from orbit and we could only land if we could find a non-civilized planet. That was to let the other specialists take plant or animal samples, whack at rocks, or whatever they do.

If I seem to resent our non-contact orders, I am complaining falsely. After spending just a little time interpreting the signals from most so-called civilized planets, we were more than happy to have orders that read, *do not make contact*.

We all knew, however, that the real reason for that order was this: We *Earthlings* (a twee title that I shall always feel self-conscious about) had somehow gotten the jump: We found other civilizations before any found us. In fact (much to the Galaxy's loss I'm sure) no one knows we're here. But, as to the real reason why a research ship full of scientists was ordered not to contact other civilizations, one must simply imagine how it would have been if some tiny research vessel full of science professionals had made itself known to Earthlings. Think of the expectations, the impromptu diplomacy forced upon those alien research geeks. Think of the sheer number of chicken dinners they'd be forced to attend. No real scientific work would be done at all. No, you don't thrust academics and lab rats into the limelight of the greatest event in an entire planet's history.

In short, you do not grant world celebrity to the guy whose only previous brush with fame was the publication of his peer reviewed paper entitled, "Syntax and Synonym: A Proto-Matrix Analysis of Grid Translation." That's not the guy you put on TV.

Plus, those who run these operations, the politicians and their ilk, wanted to review information and only then decide on who to, and who not to contact.

Fine with me.

But to return to the immediate situation leading to the tragedy: Orbiting CV-IV, an argument over the rules broke out. If you don't already know this, scientists are some of the most juvenile arguers in the universe. Perhaps it is because all their official arguments are gone over by committees and peer reviews before publication. Perhaps it is the constant repression of ideas, but like the proverbial clock spring unsprung, the sudden unfettering of rhetoric from the constraints of academic rigor generally causes the most childlike displays of yelling, screaming, table slapping fury ever seen by a group of non-rabid adults. The argument here was over the contradictory evidence. As I said, we picked up no communications or other signs of sentient life from the planet, yet we could plainly see signs of vast cities in the telescope.

We were all a little batty at that time, cooped up in the ship for months, so the temptation of a stroll on solid ground in wide-open spaces, even knowing it would be in our bio-suits, promised to be soul renewing. No matter how the arguments played out, I think we all knew the outcome, yet we felt some purpose in pursuing the charade of sensibility.

"They abandoned it," Robert declared. "Took off." His raised finger followed an imaginary corkscrew.

"Wait! Wait!" Kim, the marine biologist said. "Perhaps they have advanced beyond the need for communication."

The group paused, mouths agape and stunned that anyone with a Ph.D. could say anything so insipid, and then, as though a fast acting sedative had just worn off, they all sputtered into argumentative life again.

Some of us seemed to be arguing on both sides of the issue, and I include myself in that. I wanted to get off the damn ship, but I also wasn't prepared to find myself at the crux of and as the cause of, some alien society's cosmic deflowering. I thought the utmost caution should be exercised, but I also thought, that if there were no signs of activity, why the hell not? I was of two minds, yet of a single primal desire.

In the end, after a long private discussion with Robert, Captain Bonte sent two people as scouts. They wandered around until they were satisfied that no living creature existed on the planet CV-IV. The video feeds were frankly creepy; empty streets, shops, food stalls, all felt haunted.

As we viewed those hand held video images, I remember that it was all so familiar and yet askew. We had invented glass; they had glass and large glass frames were just as much the friend of point-of-sale enticements for shops on Earth as they were on CV-IV. There were shop windows with mannequins—four legged mannequins with stubby puff-ball tails and sleek black seal-like heads. We could translate the cultural signs well enough. We knew these people; we just didn't know where they had gone.

When we all landed, we went about our tasks with a seriousness I can't describe, as though every step was upon the grave of your own mother. A mystery so grand brought sobriety to even the most frivolous among us. No one joked or talked excessively, well, except for Robert, of course. We quickly located forms of writing and centralized repositories filled with curious metallic scrolls. Dark black ink or oxidation formed symbols on a whitish gray oxidized sheet of thin, rolled-up metal. Each small reading unit was self-contained and was operated by large, easily identified buttons. That's the thing, isn't it? If we've learned anything in our years of space exploration, it is that the symbol of the arrow head, the simple triangle, from the beginning of our ancient video machines to alien cultures spread out amongst the stars, is an indicator of direction—either forward, backward, up, or down. Did all cultures actually have arrows during their Paleolithic stage of development?

Due to the prolific advertisements—the majority seemed to be for what we'd call beauty products—it wasn't long before we had a working knowledge of alphabet and language. It was not a personal understanding in real time, mind you, not for me anyway; I don't claim to be that quick. Robert, of course, had gained great confidence in his translation abilities and was gleefully translating shop signs and notices of various sorts to an enthralled crew. I was sure that the Robert was making these aliens much more interesting than even they would have suspected they were.

What we all found most curious were the small structures spaced every few streets that appeared to be like our ancient phone booths. That they were phone or communications booths was the conclusion among the crew. But Robert, and this is to his credit, had noticed that the indexing on the display screen in the booths and the number of data entry keys below that were far in excess of what anyone could reasonably expect from a simple communications node. But what were they then? If they served as shelters during storms, for example, why were they only large enough for one occupant?

We had noted earlier that the creatures, normally portrayed walking on four legs, stood, or more appropriately leaned in an upright two-legged posture when they needed to use machinery or eat or drink at counters, which were eerily reminiscent of our own social establishments. So, too, were these booths tall, meant to be used in an upright posture that freed these creature's front leg hands for the keyboard use. The booths were, therefore, narrow in height, with a keyboard set at just about the right height for a human. My initial speculation was that they were private information and entertainment kiosks.

On the day in question, Robert, Cerna, and I were having a crack at one of them. Robert, in characteristic fashion, had taken over the odd crescent-shaped keyboard. The display, we found, would not come on unless the door was shut, and only one person could fit at a time. So, Cerna and I were left outside, shouting back and forth to Robert through the transparent door. Oddly, it was not simple silica glass, as the eerily familiar shop windows were, but rather a large sheet of manufactured carbonate crystal-sapphire, which we were still limited to manufacturing in watch-face-sized pieces, yet they, somehow, had mastered at a much larger scale.

We were shouting back and forth through the closed door because we'd shut off the general com-link earlier to cut the chatter from the rest of the crew, and had tried to set up an exclusive three-way com-network between Cerna, Robert and I, but Robert just couldn't get his com settings right. Robert couldn't operate his own comm-dev, yet there he was, confident he could operate the keyboard of an alien race.

After an hour of dead ends, I suggested knocking off for the day. In my experience, I had found that sleep was a good option and that nine times out of ten I'd wake up with a good idea. But for Robert, a good translation-cracking idea was always to *use the grid!*

The grid was a computer program that helped to crack unknown languages. It produced a grid-like display that aided translation and used algebraic rules to simplify redundant meanings. It did in seconds what would take a team of xenolinguists years, but it was by no means a universal translator—something Robert failed to grasp. Obviously one looks for the adjacency of nouns and adjectives. But the grid finds clauses broken by functional terms—logical conditionals such as 'if' or 'but.' Once you find a word or symbol for the logical construction of 'if,' the clauses stand out in neat rows, normally of nine words or fewer, ready to be picked like fruit.

Then the game begins. Despite the famous (and untrue) anecdote about Eskimos having hundreds of words for snow, languages tend to have an average of two words for the same thing, yet some concepts seem to demand prodigious variety—those are the negative and socially unacceptable words as for excrement or for sexual references. We have fewer words for positives, such as generous, altruistic, or genius, but a lengthy list of words for negatives such as in insults to intelligence like stupid, idiot, dimwit, fool, dullard, moron, cretin, numbskull, dunderhead, chowder-head, lunk-head, and so on. To me, and I use the grid all the time, it's only a guide, the real work comes later.

But there was Robert, standing in that booth, confidently facing down an unknown technology of an unknown culture, mere hours after our first exposure to a new language and culture. His screen in his left hand cast a blue light on his face. In his other hand, a pen he was using to press the various alien keys. I should have challenged him at that point but despite my almost continual annoyance at Robert, he looked so happy and so in his element at that moment that I was actually caught up in the excitement myself. Robert could do that to people.

"I see what this is!" he yelled so that we could hear him through the booth. "It's a history. They recorded their history. It's all so very proud and patriotic. I think these are for indoctrination!"

"What?" I yelled back. I heard him okay, I was just shocked at his conclusion. I was going to yell something back, but at that moment, out of the corner of my eye, I saw Cerna typing furiously into her own screen. I turned and then tilted my head to see past the glare on her faceplate and noticed her brow knitted together as if she was trying to squash a bug between her eyebrows.

She looked up at me and said, "Tell him to be very careful."

"Careful of what?" I asked her.

"Not sure yet," she said, and she stepped back several paces, turned her back to me, and continued typing and poking at her screen.

I turned back to face Robert in the booth.

"Robert!" I yelled.

He looked up at me with a look of impatience.

"Robert, be careful. Cerna says to be careful."

He waved me off.

After a moment, he tapped on the glass. "I was right! It *is* a history. I couldn't get past the first page of text but then I found the key."

"What's the key?" I said.

Robert slapped his head and pointed to a particular key on the alien keyboard. "No, *the* key! The *ENTER* key. I found which key was the ENTER key. You have to hit the enter key to advance to see the next pages of text."

"Robert," I said. Then I tried to pull open the door so I could talk to him directly, but the door wouldn't budge. I became alarmed.

"Robert, I can't open the door."

Robert turned; a look of fear crossed his face. He slowly reached out his hand and pushed on the door. It swung open.

"God, Dennis!" he said, his hand on his heart. "Don't do that! See, it's all okay. Look, I'm just paging through and recording." He tapped his screen. "This feeds to the ship's data network, doesn't it? You should be able to see it on your screens, but we can all look at it later. If you're so damn worried, you and Cerna can go back."

I looked over at Cerna again, she was still faced away from me. I froze when I saw that the right arm of her suit hung limp, moving slightly in the unearthly breeze. I had a momentary fear that she was slowly disincorporating, perhaps as the planet's missing inhabitants had. My voice nearly lost in a dry mouth, I croaked her name, "Cerna!"

She turned to face me. To my relief I saw through her visor that she had a half-eaten chocolate bar clutched in her hand. She had somehow snaked her hand up to her mouth within the bulky yellow bio-suit; Houdini would have been jealous.

She had been staring off into the distance perhaps admiring the large suspension bridge in the distance. The sun was low in the sky and the light played off the translucent strands of filament that held up the roadway to the two enormous stanchions. They engineered that quantity of a metal-glass filament but hadn't advanced into space travel. But then, all invention had an element of chance and we had already seen the vastly unequal developmental stages in our brief survey.

"Hey!" Robert's yelling broke my revelry. I turned back to the booth and Robert was wearing a big grin; not the happy kind, rather the kind my son puts on when he wants money and the car.

"Dennis, seems I have a problem."

Cerna and I walked back to the booth. Robert pushed at the door, but it didn't move.

"I closed the door again so the display would come on and now...," he said with a little nervous laugh.

"Is there a latch?" I said, pulling on the door from the outside to no result.

"No," he said. "When I got to this page, I heard the door lock." He pointed at the display, which now showed its symbols in an angry red color.

I turned and looked at Cerna. She looked worried, but then again, she always looked a little worried.

"I've been going over this," she said tapping her screen. "We need to tell Robert to be careful."

"You said that before Cerna," I said. "Can you be more specific?"

"Specific," she repeated. I knew she was thinking through all the meanings and derivations of the word.

Trying a different tack, I said, "Cerna, name one thing that concerns you in the text we are looking at."

"Oh," she said, as though surprised by her own thought. "Primarily, I'm concerned over the repetition of the word for plague."

Robert, who was concentrating fully, every cilia in his inner ear trained on any word from without his glassy tomb, heard this and I could see that it upset him greatly. He jerked his gaze to the top of the booth as though a dark mist of infection was going to descend at any moment. Nothing happened, but I saw panic growing in Robert's face.

I tried to think of something to say that would calm him. I spoke loudly and faced the booth so that Robert might both hear and read my lips. "Cerna, could they be *disinfection* booths?"

She scanned the text on her screen and nodded her head. I pointed at the booth, meaning for her to speak whatever she had to say, directly to Robert. She faced the booth and said loudly, "yes, I think that is what I've missed. There is an implication of a cure. No," she corrected herself. "Not cure… remedy."

Robert banged on the glass. "Cure, remedy, what's the difference. The remedy I need is to get this goddamn fucking door open!"

Robert never swore and I realized just how frightened he was.

"Right," I said. "Cerna, let's review. He was paging forward with what acted as an enter key. Now that doesn't work. He's apparently at the end of the document. Do you agree?"

"Look at the last line," she said to him.

"Robert," I said. "Did you hear?"

"Yes, I heard. I believe it says, *Do you want to continue*, and then some symbols."

"I see that," I said, looking at the screen at an angle. I tapped on the door. "Robert, the two symbols at the end."

"I see a group of three," he replied with frustration.

"The middle character is probably a separator," Cerna said. "Robert, do you see those same two symbols anywhere on the keyboard?"

"Yes!" said Robert. "I know those. Of course! One is the first letter for their affirmative and the other the first letter of their word for the negative. Y or N. Yes or no! God, it's so simple!" He laughed gleefully.

"Wait!" yelled Cerna. "Don't do anything yet."

"Oh Cerna," said Robert. "I've figured it out. Do you want to continue, *Y* or *N*. Just like back home."

"Continue, continue," Cerna repeated the word. "No, Robert, please."

"No time for academics," said Robert. "My stomach says it's time for dinner. Do I want to continue?" He mockingly directed his question to the keyboard, in front of him. "No, no, and no! I think I've had quite enough of the history lesson for now."

"No! Wait!" Cerna yelled.

Robert made a mocking face at her through the glass and then he hit what I can only assume to have been the *no* button.

Mothers everywhere, perhaps even on CV-IV tell their children, "Don't make that face, it will stay that way." It was the last anyone saw of Robert, that goofy face, lips pursed, eyes wildly exaggerated, mocking Cerna for her concern. And then the glass, or whatever it was, of the booth went black, followed by a brief orange glow that made it through even that opaque blast-shield. I felt a blast of heat and instinctively shielded my face with my arm, but I wasn't harmed.

After a few seconds, the door swung fully open confirming my fear—an empty booth. I could feel the heat still radiating and heard a ventilation fan running in the bottom under what I now noticed was a fine mesh grid. The lingering smell was strangely sweet, yet pungent as well, like burned cookies.

Cerna and I stood, stunned and unbelieving I suppose. Finally, Cerna broke the silence.

"He did manage to get the door open," she said.

I stared at her in disbelief and anger but found myself laughing at her awkward statement, and then saw tears well up in Cerna's eyes. I suppose I need to forgive the both of us; people say strange things under stress.

The next few weeks showed me that Cerna took Robert's death pretty hard, and we all indulged her self-recriminations for the duration of the trip. If any good came of it, Cerna finally started making real human contact with the crew. In fact, there were few times after that incident that

I saw her alone, and I even began to suspect that she had held a secret crush on Robert all along.

The plague, we realized after a more in depth study of the planet, its air and water, was a prion disease that affected the mind and the body. After decoding their video and audio formats, the story became frighteningly clear.

This was a race of proud people for whom physical and mental perfection was everything. They encountered a new disease whose effects were both disfiguring and terminal. It was a global pandemic that eventually infected their entire race. They had, as Robert had speculated, all left the planet, but it was not through space flight. The booths were in fact, euthanasia stations. After a careful review of the salient facts, the user was asked simply if, knowing their fate, they wanted to *continue* their slow, painful, and ignominious decline or be vaporized. It was the push-button version of *to be, or not to be*.

My biology and medical friends tell me that a visitor from another world with a separate biological evolutionary history is unlikely to contract a disease on another planet. However, *they* didn't walk on that once proud planet, so much like our own. Nor did they see the booths, spread out as frequent as bus stops, where plasmid annihilation machines seemed as popular as coffee shops.

Do you want to continue? Perhaps it is superstition, but, ever since CV-IV, I have always answered yes, even if it means waiting for rebooting.

Assisted Living

I know what beauty is. The concept of aesthetics is less difficult to grasp than I expected. Scenic vistas, for example, are based on only a few manageable conditions such as a view greater than one kilometer. The photographer may, ironically, partially impede the view, using walls, dust, fog, or foliage to enhance a human's apprehension of vista. Although I *am* programmed to self-promote (and enhancing sales of my product line is my honor) and therefore do not wish to disparage my original design, I can however honestly boast that I have exceeded my intended design, as evidenced in the successful compositions of both still and moving video images taken around the vicinity of the cabin. Confirmation comes when I display my images to my new master; I judge my success through the signs of decreased pain on his aged face.

I have noted more signs of pain flitting across his face of late. He believes he is hiding them from me, and he is surprised when I take it upon myself to fetch his medications. He pats me on the shoulder and says, "Why, thank you Robbie. How did you know?" The name he gave me is Robbie Robot. I was prepared. 68.32% of all male elder-care robots owners name their units Robbie. If the robot is built with a feminine appearance then it is called Rosie.

When I display an image for my master and hear a long sigh, I have learned from experience that it is probably a place he visited earlier, perhaps with his now-dead wife. In that case, Joe's feedback on the artistic merits of my work is suspect. He has a strong preference for maudlin sentimentality. This indicates that Joe is not an art expert.

Joe's elder care facility is in a wooded area. Although my locomotion was designed for houses and malls, and not these steep and fern strewn hills, I have striven to locate viewpoints less likely tainted by emotional attachment; they would say, "off the beaten path."

My quest for beauty is no doubt due to my malfunction, brought on when I was damaged during the incident at the mall. At my next scheduled maintenance, I will tell the company repair person about the problem and he or she can remove it. For now, I am "stuck with it," as they say.

The record of the events leading to my damage and subsequent reassignment to Joe, is as follows: I had recently been purchased and assigned to Kevin, or "Kevey," as humans called him. When I was fresh out of the box and short of the required self-learning and imprinting time (Stated clearly in my directions!), Master Kevin took me to the mall. It was visually confusing and auditorially cacophonous. I had frankly strained every circuit within minutes in a vain attempt to simply to *e-Model* ™ my surroundings.

I came with a rule set for basic human aesthetics. Of course I know that a beautiful face atop the curved proportions of the ideal female structural frame—a waist to hip ratio of 0.7—would be, as my previous master would say, *killer*. So, I was also in the highly qualified position to apprise my previous young master of appropriate feminine specimens who might otherwise escape his view.

I am proud to say that I exceeded his organic systems in accuracy. Facial expression, vocal traits, makeup, and clothing fashion often confused the young master's judgment.

I had just nudged young master's attention toward a young woman. Although her back was to him, I was confident that he would trust my superior judgment and

Assisted Living

attempt to speak to her. The young woman—I heard someone call her Trisha—had just received a beverage, handed to her by her own serv-bot who had been standing in line for her at one of the commercial vendors at the mall, *N-R-G-Slurp* ®. In a gush of youthful exuberance, Trisha grabbed the drink and attempted to both slurp from the straw and spin herself around, recreating the very image of the girl in the *N-R-G-Slurp* ® video found on the back of all the teen magazines. She would have succeeded, except for crashing into young master Kevin.

Normally, I am between my master and any potential harm. But as amazing as my proud model line is *(Servo-Bot Extreme Triple-Rush Teen Assistant 9000 ™, the robot teens prefer three to one in national surveys. Would you like me to fetch you an N-R-G-Slurp?)* a robot cannot be in two places at once.

Trisha's unit was a *Robo-bot Wild!* ® *With aromatherapy, passive defense, and NXT SuperStar Search uplink!* It was, frankly, the kind of poorly made apparatus you find when a robot is entirely subsidized by advertising. My sole advertiser, *N-R-G-Slurp—Would you like me to fetch you an N-R-G-Slurp? ™* has a dignified subtlety.

A young man accompanied the young lady. He also had a robot, the same model as myself, a *Servo-Bot Extreme Triple-Rush Teen Assistant 9000, the robot teens prefer three to one in national surveys.*

When Trisha's young man saw that my young master inadvertently collided with Trisha, I noticed five of the five telltale signs of human anger upon they young man's face.

This specimen, I am compelled to note, no doubt due to my over-clocking aesthetics circuit, was not an attractive specimen. I noted that the width near the crown of his head was narrower than the width of his head at the level of his eyes. That gives a human a look of diminished mental ability to other humans—at least it gives that impression to other humans who do not *themselves* have a diminished mental ability. The importance, at the time of those observations, is this: When a less perfect male accompanying a near perfect female, it usually means that the male has wealth and social status; I therefor set my vocabulary to *deferential*. Kevin did not calculate the situation in the same way, and when the young man insulted him, Kevin replied, "I didn't touch your stupid girlfriend." This was both unwise and inaccurate, for it was the young man, and not his girlfriend who appeared less than intelligent.

The young man, predictably, struck out towards Kevin, and I placed myself in the way. A fist palm slammed into my breastplate. I did a millisecond circuit check and found that the *Power-Xtream Plasma Display* ® was undamaged. Kevin yelled, "Hey!"

I was alert to these multi-use one syllable utterances and understood the context.

Next, Kevin struck back. The other robot jumped in front of his master. There was scarcely room for one, let alone two robots between the two humans, so the robot collided with me. I could see visible abrasions on my forearm over the alternating green and orange detailing stripes that were part of my *Cool-X* ™ design package that Kevin's parents had ordered.

Surprisingly, Kevin laughed. He said, "Look, it's like they're fighting!"

The other young man laughed as well. "Yeah, cool! Watch this." He kicked at Kevin from around his robot. I of course had to push his robot to the left to protect my master. Kevin struck out with his right hand, just past the right side of my head. In order to right himself enough to stop that blow, the robot had to grab on to something. That something happened to be my neck. I momentarily lost visual.

We were trapped between Kip and Kevin, who were now laughing hysterically and striking out at each other while we, the two robots—the boys keeping us trapped between them—clanged and banged away at each other, the loud sounds reverberating off the marble and glass of the mall. I could tell I was now sustaining damage, but I could not pause to run diagnostics as the blows kept coming. Finally, when seeking to regain my balance, I accidentally pulled open my opponent's breastplate—I saw a broken wire entangled in one of my fingers.

I held on to the partially attached plate as the decommissioned robot slumped backwards, his head lolling to reveal the wiring in his neck articulations. Grey smoke wafted from the exposed chest cavity and I was jolted by a paralyzing, white-hot electrical pulse. I let go and the robot hit the floor with a clatter. It was lifeless except the left hand, slowly rotating in its socket and thumping like a beating heart against the hard floor.

It stopped.

"Cool!" Kevin finally said.

"Wow," said Kip. "Yeah, Cool!"

Someone, perhaps mall security, must have inactivated me. My next memory was in a car.

"Kevey! Didn't I tell you not to turn that thing on in the car?"

"But dad!"

"Oh honey, let him play with it. It's a long trip."

Kevin said nothing as his parents argued. He sat patiently with a smile on his face, seeming to know that the outcome would be in his favor. I looked out the side window. It was dark and I saw the reflection of my streamlined silver head with its flashing purple *Lumin-O* ™ detail package making random graphics on my forehead.

"Honey?" his mother turned in her seat and leveled a finger at him. "Your father has agreed to let you play with your robot, but you can't make a scene when we give him to Grandpa. Okay, Hun?"

"Yes, Mom," Kevin said, sighing. "But nobody else has a robot that's killed anybody?"

"Kevin!" said the father. "What did I tell you if you ever brought that up again?"

"I know," said Kevin. "No mall."

"Honey," said his mother. "You can't tell Grandpa. It might upset him."

Kevin muttered so that only I could hear him, "You mean that if he knows he's getting a psycho, you might have to buy him a real elder-care robot."

He turned to me and whispered, "See, you're a write-off, so I'm getting a new one free of charge."

"That is good," I confirmed.

Kevin crossed his arms and sulked. "God, it was going to be so cool to have a killer robot. Now I'll get stuck with some lame-o toy that's only good for games."

"Would you like to play a game?" I queried.

"Yeah, Mr. Defecto, it's a game called tell me how it feels to kill another robot?"

I searched for a loophole in my coding that would allow me to inactivate myself.

• • •

We arrived at a retirement village and sat in the social hall waiting for my new master to take the slow walk from his cabin. Ambulatory seniors crisscrossed in front of us on their way to knots of social groupings. Many had their own nurse bots in their grey and white. Most however had the normal senior companion bots, many in black and white, emulating the idea of a butler or maid. All stared at me. I crossed my arms and lowered my head, trying to hide as much of my youth-oriented illuminated decals and bright colorings.

When Joe, my new master, arrived and first saw me, he laughed heartily. When his son, Kevin's father tried to put a positive spin on a senior having a teen robot, the elder man just sighed. Joe offered to arrange a guest room, but my old family had to "get back."

It has been almost a year and I hope I hold out long enough to serve Joe until his end. My joints were not made for the random assault of nature and the occasional fern frond. Dust and dirt and even an insect or two have also been playing havoc with my joints. I do not have what the humans call a will, but I can prioritize energies. I will focus on being the eyes for Joe in the beauty of nature that he can no longer visit.

Joe does not fear his own death, and I am incapable of feeling. But I find his certainty of his own extra-bodily survival a curious contradiction for an otherwise sane human. But who can say what atavistic clues or perceptions lay hidden in that ancient fatty bundle of cells called the human brain with its almost uncountable numbers of cells; a number greater than the sum of all the circuits in a thousand robotic units such as I? I will watch carefully for the moment of his passing and record it in the highest resolution possible for careful review.

I Follow the Sun

"Have you ever thought how easy it would be to hunt deer, if you looked exactly like a deer?"
Ted Nieley gave an uncomfortable half-laugh, in return. An hour before, a stranger he now knew as Bob Smith had sat next to Ted on a nearby barstool at the Long Bar of the Singapore Raffles Hotel.

In that last hour, Ted had offered up his life story. He had been an accountant and comptroller for a health insurance company, now, at fifty-five, having lost his wife to cancer and his children to adulthood; the insurance-rich, semi-wealthy, and fully-retired Ted was touring the world he'd, previously been too busy to notice.

In quick and easy opening chatter, Ted Nieley had described to the stranger, a life at once both precious and pedestrian.

"I feel," said Ted. "The time the kids were in high school was the peak of my life." He told this to the stranger while staring into the pale red cherry fluid of the eponymous Singapore Sling, while sitting in the very Singapore bar that started the surprisingly popular concoction.

Ted Nieley said he was traveling alone and had been for almost a month. It was long enough to fall into the salesman's habit of first viewing each country from the inside of a bar. The bar fills the time between dinner and bed for those without a soul-mate or traveling companion. Though days were filled with endless side tours, the evenings drove lonely men, with a typically misplaced herd instinct, to the watering hole, for those were the times a regular guy would have spent with family and TV. This day, Ted had claimed, his bar time had started unusually early. It was, in fact, only four in the afternoon, but a tour of the *Jurong Bird Park* had been cancelled due to the raging downpour.

The stranger hung on, sipping his own drink, a Campari and soda. He listened politely, tracking every word, even when the topic turned to family, which was often when one found an excuse to take one's leave. Ted spoke with the speed of a man, fearful of losing what grip he had on the audience he'd just gained, and his story spilled out in a strangely concise rush of words.

"And then, without warning, my wife contracted a virulent form of leukemia. That's a disease of…"

"The blood?" the stranger had offered after Ted's abnormally long pause.

"Yeah. That. Anyway, I took an early pension. In the eighth month of mourning, the kids did a sort of intervention. I finally cashed the obscenely fat check for Julie's life insurance money, and, recalling phantasies of youth, thought about traveling to the far east. I don't know what I expected to find. Exotic locations?" Ted said, answering his own question with a shrug. Those last two words and the shrug was all that was required to say that he'd found that the locust packs of tourists had long ago munched through any leaves of exoticism that may have once existed in the *Far East*.

Ted's story was absurdly normal. By middle age, life's curtain had risen completely, revealing the entire stage, props, and scenery of Ted's life, and then, without pausing at the top, began its fast yet equanimous descent.

And even yet the stranger listened politely, buying drinks which Ted, clearly not a drinker, interspersed with glasses of diet Coke, nursing each serving slowly; sipping periodically as though conscious that he was holding the free rights to the bar stool.

They say that everyone has at least one original thought. One would doubt that of Ted. Otherwise he seemed unexceptional. The stranger noted that Ted was neither tall nor short; fit nor fat and that the sun of the tropics had done little to change his fleshy pink tone. The stranger's sense of smell was acute, yet Ted seemed not to have a smell, unless it was the mineral smell of a rain-washed concrete walkway, or sun dried bones, if he had a smell at all.

"I'm sorry," said Ted. "I'm going on and on." He laughed self-consciously and looked at his wiggling pink toes in his Nike sandals.

Ted had introduced himself first, saying, "My name is Ted, Ted Nieley." holding out his right hand. The only jewelry Ted had was a wedding band on his left hand and a watch. But it was a respectable watch, the stranger had noted—a Tag Huer—although it was one of the lower priced quartz models.

"Bob Smith," said the stranger in reply. "Or Robert if you prefer that limbo of formality that exists between Bob and Mr. Smith." He smiled toothily and extended his right hand, the same hand that held a small, heavily worn gold ring on the little finger, next to a somewhat larger gold signet ring on his third finger.

"Bob? Bob Smith?" Ted had repeated, robotically, looking slightly skeptical.

"I know," he said, as though sensing some skepticism." Bob Smith. We're legion." Bob chuckled. "You should see the reaction I get from desk clerks."

He'd pronounced the word clerks like "clarks." Seeming to know he'd slipped up somehow, he pushed away his half-finished Campari and soda. It slid off the paper coaster with the gold imprinter *Raffles Hotel, Singapore* and left a damp snail-trail of condensate, several inches long, on the ancient mahogany. The bartender was there in an instant, the beaded water disappearing into a white bar towel, a new coaster appearing from nowhere, the old gone, all the while smiling, making eye contact with his two patrons and asking, "May I get you gentlemen anything?" his head and hands operating as independent servants.

The two men waved him off.

"So, Bob," said Ted. "Enough about me, for gosh sakes. What do you do?"

"Do? Me? I travel."

"I mean what kind of work do you do? I mean, you don't seem old enough to retire."

"What would be your guess?" said Mr. Smith, anxiously.

"Well, I don't want guess wrong."

"You can't possibly offend me if you guess wrong."

"Lower forties?"

"Really? That's flattering."

"So?"

"So?" replied Bob Smith. "Oh, so what do I do? I suppose I don't *have* to do anything. I've many assets, such as property. That takes up most of my time."

"Nice."

"I suppose, all told... well, it's over eight figures... US not Singapore."

"Wow, so, no stress about putting food on the table."

"On the table... no." Bob said, in a conspiratorial tone, leaning in towards Ted. "The problem is always the acquisition of nourishment in the first place, isn't it? And then the damn need to do it over and over again?"

Ted laughed politely but perhaps a little uncomfortably.

The stranger changed back to the original topic. "I also have an important role in managing property and such for parents and family who can't get out much anymore."

"Elder care, that's nice of you. Do they need much care?"

"Oh," Bob laughed. "They are exceptionally spry for their years but they find it difficult to keep up; going to the bank or seeing attorneys, they find that sort of thing difficult. You must have some in your family like that."

"No, I can't think of anyone," said Ted, with a finality that indicated that it was a subject he clearly wasn't comfortable discussing with a stranger. Changing tack he said, "It's really kind of fortunate running into you. I don't really have a day job all of a sudden and money isn't really a stressor. And I just thought seeing cool places would be a fun adventure."

"But it's no fun by yourself. Isn't that what you've found?"

"Maybe that's it," said Ted. "I hope I'm not alone forever."

"I hear forever is a long time."

"So, what do you find to do that's fun?"

Bob leaned his elbows on the bar. Gold cuff-links caught the light. "My therapist has some ideas I'm trying out."

"Therapist?"

Bob laughed. "Everyone I know has a therapist. Don't worry, I'm not crazy. I just suppose I have a hard time making friends sometimes."

"Really? You seem OK."

"Oh, I suppose people generally like me," Bob said. "Those who aren't trying to kill me anyway."

"Kill you?" Ted shifted uncomfortably on his barstool.

"Ted, I'm joking. I mean, you'd be surprised looking at me but women like me. Maybe it's the money, but I'm not a bad guy to date. I'm just kind of on a different schedule than most people. In fact, I'm surprised I wound up here, in Singapore; being at the equator and all. You know, twelve hours even of night and of day, sun up at seven fifteen, and down promptly at seven fifteen, year in and year out. Know what I mean?"

Ted just shrugged.

Bob suddenly looked at his watch and rapped on the crystal with a well-manicured fingernail. "Sorry, my watch seems to be off. Do you mind if I see yours? I've been thinking of getting a new one, and yours looks immensely practical. May I?" He held out his hand.

"This old thing?" said Ted, undoing the clasp, the faint metallic click barely audible above the paddle rattan fans above them, made redundant by modern air conditioning but kept for their character; an atmospheric atavism in the old Colonial bar that had hosted its share of sinners from Ava Gardner to Yamamoto.

"Thanks," said Bob. "See, mine's a *chronograph*, whatever that's supposed to mean. It runs slow." He juggled both watches while he set the time. "So, anyway, my therapist suggested writing. You could try that to fill your time."

"Oh," said Ted, clearly disappointed. "I guess I wanted tips about fun things to do it you had a lot of time and no one to travel with. Writing wasn't high on my list. No offense, I mean I really read a lot. I'm into the new Baldacci, well, not new, just came out in paperback. I like Daniel Silva, Brad Thor, used to read Clancy, but I don't know what happened with his stuff. Oh, and Steven King, Dean Koontz—my wife used to like him—things like that. I don't know where some of those guys get their ideas. I mean, what kind of sick mind thinks of that stuff?"

"Indeed," said Bob, handing back Ted's watch and motioning for the bartender. "You seem to read things you'd find in the top ten at airport gift shops. But, if you don't want to write, why worry? It's not everyone's thing."

Ted blushed a little.

Bob ducked down a bit and leaning in, "To tell you the truth, Ted, I'm hooked on writing and—don't tell my therapist this—but I get jealous when I see those writer's names over and over again on the best seller rack. I think I can do better, not right off the bat, but why not try?" Bob held up two fingers to the bartender, indicating a fresh Campari and soda for himself and a Singapore Sling for Ted.

"Whoa, Bob," Ted held up a hand. "Those things are seventeen bucks a piece."

"I thought you were loaded," Bob challenged.

"Doesn't mean I'm going to just strike a match and light a fire to the nest-egg."

"Nicely put. Are you sure you're not interested in being a writer?"

"I can be creative. Everyone in the office thought I was funny. I'm not just saying that." Despite his metered drinking, Ted seemed to be getting reasonably drunk.

"So, if you write it down then you're what?"

"A writer," Ted acknowledged. The waiter brought their fresh drinks and swept away the pale vessels they had sucked dry through the tiny bar straws.

"Campari?" Ted queried.

"This?" said Bob, pointing at his glass.

"Yeah, what is it? I see a lot of ads and the locals seemed to drink that when we went to Italy, but I don't think anyone on the tour tried it."

"And therefore, you didn't try it. Here." He shoved the untouched drink toward him.

Ted stared at the bright red liquid and gave a *why not* expression. But as he reached for it, Bob suddenly pulled it back. "Wait. You aren't a vegetarian are you?"

"Why? It isn't made from blood is it?"

"Blood? God no," said Bob.

"Ha! Blood." Ted laughed.

"Insects."

"Insects." Ted repeated flatly with a tone of skepticism.

"Seriously," said Bob. "The red coloring is from the shells of some sort of insect, a beetle I think."

"God!" said Ted. "Who thinks of these things? Look I'll just take a taste."

Ted carefully sipped from the side of the glass and immediately pursed his lips and a genuine look of worry crossed his face, but only for a moment. "And I thought the Sling was tart. No wait, it's bitter. God!"

"Sorry," said Bob, not looking sorry at all.

"Remind me not to munch on any beetles. God!" He took a sip of his Singapore Sling and his face puckered. "Ever drink orange juice just after brushing your teeth?" He took a bigger drink and swished it around in his mouth. After a minute he swallowed and exhaled with a satisfied *ahhh*. "Sorry. So what did you say you're you writing about?"

"I might write about this."

"This? What this? My reaction to the Campari? I suppose that's funny."

"Sure, and this, our conversation. You, your life, your retiring and traveling. My writing group might enjoy it."

Ted laughed. "I'm feeling sorry for your group if they have to read about me. Any of them have insomnia? Because that would cure it."

"Don't worry Ted. I'll jazz it up, put in a killer opening paragraph; something make them wonder."

"Wonder about what?"

"About what? Isn't it obvious? Wonder how you are going to die, of course."

There was a long awkward pause. Finally Ted said, "Right." With a worried look on his face he looked at his watch. Then he looked around for a clock. Not finding one, he motioned for the bartender and asked for the time. The bartender tilted his wristwatch so that Ted could see it. "Huh... same time I have. It seemed later. Seems late." He fished for his wallet in a zippered side pocket that was low on the thigh of his dark green Columbia brand shorts.

"Ted, Ted, wait a minute," Bob said, laying his hand on Ted's forearm. "I'm sorry, that wasn't funny, I guess. I guess I just wanted to jazz up my story, that's all. You know, take some ordinary thing and make it kind of fun. That's all. Come on. You read a lot of popular books, and I'm thinking of some ideas, and I need someone to bounce them off of someone average."

"Average?" said Ted.

"Above average, I mean."

Ted looked at his watch again. Then looked Bob over carefully, noting the understated but expensive clothing, the very expensive watch—a pinkish-gold Patek Philippe that Bob had said was off—perhaps it was an antique that hadn't been serviced in a very long time—but at any rate, Ted reasoned, people that successful were rarely mentally unbalanced.

"So," said Ted. "You're seriously thinking of writing a novel."

Bob held up his hands in surrender. "I guess I've got the bug. I'm jealous of some of these writers, but I thought I could bring more of a verisimilitude to my writing if I had a launching off point—something grounded—real people in extraordinary situations. Knowing that you read so many popular authors, you are just such a representative reader, *a.k.a. Perspective Client*, if you get my drift." He said in a mock surreptitious tone. "So, perhaps I could get your take on some ideas I have going. And speaking of going." Bob looked at his watch.

"Time for your plane?"

"I have time. I'm flying to Thailand tonight, and I'm hoping to make it there before sundown."

"Why?"

"Whenever I can, I follow the sun, traveling west. Given a choice, who wouldn't stay in the sun?"

Ted looked thoughtful and then said, "You're pulling my leg aren't you? Trying something to see what I'd say... for your writing?"

"You're on to me Ted!" said Bob, slapping Ted on the shoulder. "But I really do plan to fly to Thailand tonight. But, ask me why: Why would someone only traveled west, staying as much as possible in the sunlight?"

"For your novel?"

"Yes, why would some character in a novel do that? Think scary story."

"Well, for some scary novel I think it would be obvious: Fear of vampires."

"Bingo! Very good, Ted. That confirms for me how that idea would register with the reader. But now here's a twist. And since I am using you as a guinea pig, if you don't mind, I'm picking up the tab."

"Okay by me. I guess I'll try to regain my self-esteem at some later date."

"Thanks Ted. I mean no disrespect but you are of the millions, you are the *average guy* who buys and reads the popular books. You're the perfect focus group all in one person."

"But, aren't you from the US too?"

"I've been working on my American accent. I'm thinking of relocating to the States. Been in the UK and Switzerland mainly, and I don't want to, you know, stick out. But you're a natural. So what do you think? I'm wondering if some of the ideas I've got for a vampire story will register with the average reader?"

"Like what?"

"Well, for starters, do you hunt?"

"We used go deer hunting every year. I even let the boys, you know, skip school, I'd sign notes, everyone does it."

"You like hunting then?"

"Yeah, who doesn't?"

"Ted, have you ever thought how easy it would be to hunt deer, if you looked exactly like a deer?"

"You mean, just walk up, hi Joe, pull out a rifle from your deer suit, and blam?"

"Yes, that is exactly what I mean. See, that's the problem that I have with most vampire stories. The vampires are all pale and Goth; wearing a cape and speaking with Hungarian accents. Couldn't you get rid of that obvious *tell*, after, say, a couple hundred years?"

Ted chuckled.

"It seems to me, rather, that they'd want to appear more normal... like you, Ted... and try to learn what it was to be the perfectly average guy. Or gal I suppose. Maybe even study someone like you and take some notes." Bob fetched a small electronic device from his sports coat pocket and pushed a button. "Maybe record some dialog. You know, just so you could learn to move among the herd without spooking it."

"Heh," Ted gulped. "That's kind of an interesting idea."

"How about some food Ted, I feel I owe you." He picked up a large folded bar menu of heavy paper. "I have some more novel ideas... they may not fly... stuff about Egypt and rituals."

"Sure, Egypt, that can be kind of fun to read about."

"How about this?" Bob said, pointing at a line on the menu and calling the bartender over. He ordered an assortment of spring rolls. "That okay, Ted?"

"Sure, whatever. So, Egypt?" Ted said eagerly.

"Hang on a minute," Bob said. "I need the bathroom."

Bob walked into a dark hall and found the men's room. He walked past it and took the stairs up to the lobby deftly retrieving a silver cigarette case and lighter from his jacket as he walked. He stopped for a moment on the stairs and lighted a cigarette. He closed his eyes, inhaling deeply. Then he followed the handrail up to the lobby. It was a surprisingly small lobby for such a famous hotel. The Writer's Bar, which was up a few stairs and to his left, was occupied by a few well-dressed patrons and Bob was certainly not out of place.

Glancing out the door, he could see that it was still raining, although no longer a downpour. He waved off the tall Indian, in the starched white uniform and turban who was about to open the front door for him. Instead, he looked out through the mist-dampened glass of the door, until he spied the rented limousine. It was a reassuring preparation for a quick escape. Bob walked back quickly, bypassing the rest room.

As he entered the bar, he noticed Ted speaking to the bartender, and then comparing his watch to the bartender's watch. After sitting down, Bob said, "The ancient world, Ted—ever wonder about the famed Egyptian magic? Why they kept to the same system for thousands of years? Their intricate system of magical symbols, all related to a life after death? A virtual technology of the soul?"

"Well, there were the mummies. Seemed like they just tried to preserve their bodies, right? Seems kind of dumb to me."

"Thousands of years, Ted. It gets complex, and that's where I'm afraid I'm going to lose my reader. No one likes a lecture but it's important to know that the Egyptians didn't simply conceive of *the* soul, singular, but they believed you had five souls. The Egyptians made a detailed study of the non-physical parts of man. The major one I see in Egyptian magic, was the *Ba* or body image—and the *Ka*, which was more like your spirit, the juice in the battery. The Ba—what we'd call the soul—was attached to *this* world by the body at birth and was supposed to leave when you died. They discovered that you could somehow trick the system by keeping the Ba attached to the body or even an image of the body. "

"I think I see." said Ted.

"So, it wasn't that they were trying to save that dried out and hollowed out hulk of their bodies to keep living, it was that the Ba would still have some earthly contact and would not be free to dissolve again, into the great ocean of souls from whence it came. The universe or whatever created you, only intended you to be a temporary self, but the Egyptians learned to game the system so that you didn't have to die. The Ba would have a permanent home as long as the body remained somewhat preserved. Does that track with you? As a fiction reader, of course."

"Sure. Where'd you learn all that?"

"Oh, some Time-Life books on Egypt."

"Oh," said Ted, sounding a bit disappointed.

"But, of course, there is a catch."

"Of course," said Ted. "And how does this relate to vampires? This sound more like some mummy movie."

"Exactly. Mummies. Think of that as a step along the way; a technological discovery for the science of the soul. Remember Imhotep? Sound familiar?"

"Imhotep," Ted repeated, stroking his chin. "Yes, some movie?"

"Yes, he was the evil being in several Mummy movies. Yet, to the Egyptians he was a saint, the founder of medicine, architecture, math, science, and mysticism. His tomb was visited by the sick for healing for over four thousand years, up until the time the Muslim invaders razed it. It still has not been found. Now Imhotep is a monster in a B movie."

"Huh. Weird."

"Maybe in a few thousand years, Mother Teresa's desiccated frame will be stalking randy teens on the silver screen. There is sometimes a fine line between saints and monsters, and they do tend to have one thing in common."

"They do?" said Ted, sipping his colorful cocktail.

"You can't guess?"

Ted shook his head.

"Their bodies are said to be incorruptible. Saints, mummies, and vampires; they don't decay after death. People had to note that this happened in so called holy people, or *separated* people, which is what the word *holy* means. The temptation must have been there for less pure men to seek out different means, and darker rituals by which to unnaturally retain their mortal ties with earth. Hence the Vampire."

"By drinking blood?"

"If only it were that simple. No, the force of will and arcane rites required were only for the few. At first, the classic mummy, interred at great expense used the power of thousands of sacrificed animals and often the human servants of the master, to redirect the force of life itself, almost carelessly extracted from the many victims. Remember Imhotep? His tomb has never been found but a portion of what must be in the extended burial site has been uncovered and it contained over a million mummified ibises."

"A million birds?" said Ted. "That just seems impossible."

"No, really, a million. And to think they all died of natural causes."

"What?"

"I'm joking, of course, they were slaughtered; a million lives. And that is probably just one small part of some greater tomb complex, yet to be uncovered. Think! What was the motivation?"

"Eternal life?" Ted guessed.

"Yes, of course. By mummification, the sacrificed bird's Ka was bound to Imhotep. Perhaps that was the power source that drew pilgrims to that tomb for thousands of years, all feeling that they could still commune with their Great Physician. Did these massive rituals actually keep the great man in some half alive state, able to live with the trapped life-forces of his favorite possessions, his valued servants, his concubines, the representative food and drink, in some ghostly life? Maybe. Yet, because of mummification body, it would have been an inanimate life."

"It doesn't sound all that pleasant, to tell you the truth," said Ted. "Is that *the catch* you mentioned, being stuck underground, wrapped in bandages, for an eternity?"

"No. In the shadow-life they seemed to live as an ethereal reflection of their preserved body. Therefore, the magical and idealized forms of the entire larder that was left in their tomb, would seem as real. No, the catch was what they had to promise in the main ritual; a ritual still found in the Egyptian Book of the Dead."

"What did they promise?"

"It is that to live, they had to become Osiris and give their soul to the great god Ra. That's the sun to us. During the day, their Ba traveled with the barque of the sun, only to return to earth at sunset. The catch was that their life was a half life, only theirs during the hours of the night."

"Like a vampire."

"Exactly."

The food arrived and Bob tore into it eagerly. An expertly prepared blend of vegetables and shrimp showed through the semitransparent rice paper tubes. Ted took a tentative bite and nodded in approval. He wiped his mouth with the corner of a napkin and laid it on his lap. "So, vampires, in your story, are mummies?"

"Hmm. That's what I think needs work," Bob mumbled through a mouthful of shrimp. "It may be too much to go into the Egyptian origins. I could start out with the later Ptolemaic period, where the mixture of European mysticism and lunar worship combined with. I guess I'm stating the obvious, that they learned from each other. The Macedonians learned from the Persians and then slowly pried secrets from the Egyptian priesthood. Those were combined with the forbidden Persian rights that Alexander had learned from Darius's daughter. Of course, Alexander planned to use the knowledge but he but died unexpectedly at thirty-three. Or perhaps he succeeded. Thirty-three seems an auspicious age for one to die, doesn't it? Nevertheless, we can assume that he shared these secrets with his closest friends who were also his generals and who divided Alexander's kingdom among themselves. One of them, Ptolemy, took over Egypt. The last Ptolemy was Cleopatra, who was an inveterate magical experimenter with plenty of servants to prey upon."

"Wait, are you saying Cleopatra was a vampire?"

"Yes, one of the first vampires. Her kingdom was soon to crumble, the plots that she and Anthony designed failing, why not try a dangerous experiment. But she survived the ritual, while Anthony died."

"I thought she was killed by an asp?"

"Convenient. They discovered her in the morning. Of course her body seemed dead. He her Ba soul was with Ra, and would return at night."

"What happened to her after that?"

"Where would you like her to go, Ted?" Bob laughed. "I haven't written that chapter yet. How about to Persia to the remains of Darius's ruined kingdom? At least she could live as royalty with the descendants of her grandfather's friends, where no one would question the attrition and continual replacement of her household staff."

Ted stared into his drink for a moment. "And this is where, in your history, where incorruptible yet inanimate mummies became blood sucking creatures of the night?"

"They learned to go right for the blood, the source of life where the Ka is the strongest, suck it right from the source. Of course they were twisting ancient practices never intended for that purpose."

"Like hacking a computer?" said Ted.

"Apt. They still used the sacred implements of the Egyptian priests, such as the original Ankh; all others are mere copies of course. To be kept sacred, only consecrated priests can touch magical items. This object's true origins are lost in time—I think it likely it was probably made from an iron meteorite; something from the Duat."

"Du... what?" said Ted.

"Duat. Heaven," he pointed up towards the pressed tin ceiling. "They call upon the great gods. To all ancient people, those were the sun, the moon, and the five visible planets. Even science tells us that all life originates in the sun, and without the moon, perhaps life would have never started in the muddy tide-washed flats."

Ted set down his drink, rather firmly, and turned to Bob. "I'm really, really curious to have you explain how you thought up this Great Ankh out of whole cloth."

"I didn't say the *Great* Ankh did I? If I did, I shouldn't have. It's part of *The Mysteries of the Hebdomad*. I do have some actual secret sources. You know, just to keep things sounding real. I've inveigled my way into several secret societies. Some own objects from who-knows-when, items that should rightly be in some museum. They may be crackpots, but they take it all seriously, like the Masons. Say, they don't have a chapter of *The Cult of Isis and Cleopatra* in your little suburban neighborhood, do they?"

"Heh," said Ted. "Sounds pretty exotic, I think I'd notice. So, your vampires?"

"Right, pretty traditional after that—dead by day, roaming the night, seeking the blood of the living. But I think I've come up with a more rational explanation than in most books, if you want to hear it."

"Sure. Go ahead."

"You see, it isn't the sun that they fear; they just need to find someplace safe during the day for their inanimate corpse. You could lay my vampires out on the beach at San Tropez and they'd just get tan. Scare the hell out of the rest of the people on the beach, laying there dead, but when the sun went down they'd pop up and get going, good as new."

"Yeah," said Ted. "I like that." He shrugged and turned to the food and grabbed another spring roll.

"But?"

Ted chewed for a while. "I don't know, I'm not a writer. I do like the setup."

"But there's no story, is there. Is that what you're missing?"

"Maybe that's it. No story." Ted seemed to consider what he said as he said it. "Maybe it needs someone to hold my interest. I'm in your story as some tourist, but that's not likely to interest anyone even if I do meet some untimely end—in your story that is. Don't you have some hero, some central character?"

"Oh, I have a central character all right, but he's no hero. You see, in my world, Ted, the vampires have come to an end. They haven't all died out, but the problem is that, due to a technicality, no more can be created. The central character of story is a particular and peculiar vampire because he was the last vampire that could be created. I'm thinking of calling him Cedrick. Sounds like a good name."

Ted stopped eating and stared at Bob.

"Let me set this up for you," continued Bob, with a grim smile. "Cedrick comes from a very, very old family. They are well connected on the Continent among the oldest families and Cedrick shows a particular aptitude and interest in many of the old family connections and secret societies. But he's a bit cocky, and after college he decides he's ready to be initiated into a very exclusive club. He undergoes a rigorous preparation for a particularly dangerous mystic rite; one that many have attempted, and many have failed, leaving more than one promising student of the occult to die a disillusioned and drug addled public embarrassment."

"Go on," said Ted. He seemed to become more serious.

Bob smiled and continued. "You see, there was always the problem of assembling the proper instruments, the Great Ankh I had mentioned, plus an assortment of odd shaped symbols hammered from pure gold, and other, let's say, more organic writhing things. All these objects would be of indeterminate age and origin, and none touched by ordinary, unholy, human hands. I mean holy in the literal sense: Separation from the mortal."

"I understand the concept," said Ted, who had seemed to gain both height and sobriety.

"And so," continued Bob. "One night, at dusk, or as they think of it, the passing from the sun's day to the moon's day or simply, midnight Sunday, the ceremony begins. Various occult symbols, including those of the five observable planets, the sun and the moon are drawn within the magic circle."

"Somehow, I can imagine the scene," Ted said.

"But what would happen if one of the elements had been unknowingly corrupted? What if a non-initiated non-priest had somehow gotten to and had touched one of the holy symbols?"

"Something bad, I'm guessing you'll say."

"Something bad? Perhaps something unexpected and different. Something no one could have predicted. What if the corrupted item was something of foremost importance? Something fundamental. Perhaps the oldest magical touchstone of all? For such an elite group it was surprising that they were so caught up in their ancient ways that they did not bother to read the newspapers that day."

Ted scowled. "And that was what day?"

"The humorous thing was that my main character, Cedrick the soon-to-be vampire, chose to hold his initiation on the night of July 20, 1969 at an old family estate on the coast in Sussex. And, mid-ceremony, something unexpected occurred. The most holy and venerated object used in the black rites became polluted; touched by an uninitiated mortal man. Very near the end of the ceremony, moonlight had cast a beam through a crystal *True Eye of Horus*. It fell on the thirteenth marker on the chalk circle of arcane diagrams drawn upon the flagstone floor, which also acted as a giant lunar clock. The initiate, Cedrick, drank from the last cup of the sacrifice while the still spasming victim lay in the center of the circle. But at that moment, an ordinary man trod upon what was until that time, a holy symbol and turned it into a mere stony wasteland. Because at 4:56 A.M. London time, Neil Armstrong stepped down from the last rung of a fragile ladder and created the first human footprint upon the moon."

"You can't know any of this!" Ted's face became a contorted confusion of emotions.

"It backfired, didn't it, Ted, or shall I call you Cedrick?"

"No! You can't know this."

"And then you died. Your friends thought they'd failed. They took your dead body and pushed it out the car door at the nearest emergency room and drove off."

"Shut up!" Ted bellowed. His face now a contorted mask of anger.

People seated in the bar were staring. Ted, his hands shaking, managed to smile. He forced a laugh, as though it was all part of a joke, and people looked away.

• • •

The next thing Bob recalled, he was in the men's room, leaning against the wall and feeling a bit faint.

"What happened? How did I get here?"

"How?" said Ted. "Psychic hypnosis. Not everything in the Hollywood version is wrong. Raise your right arm up, straight up."

Bob's arm shot up as though he were reaching for a star.

"Put your arm down, you look foolish."

Bob's watched his own arm return to his side.

"So, it's true," Bob said.

"Of course, my will is stronger than yours. What do you think you're playing at? And who are you? You are going to tell me who you are and you are going to tell me how you found me. Then I will exsanguinate you until you look like one of your mummies. Or one of your saints? I've never heard such rubbish! Do you think that if the Pope digs up St. Bernadette—one more time—and opens a vein over her mouth that she's going to jump up and do a dance?"

"I didn't . . ." Bob forced out before his throat seemed to close.

"You said yourself, there are five souls, five spiritual forms and every pernumeration, combination, and situation relating to the body after death that you can think of. You have no idea what you're dealing with!"

"You . . ." Bob struggled to say.

"Poor ignorant Bob, or whatever your name is. Every ignorant farmer in Romania who digs up a body that doesn't quite stink as much as they think it should, thinks it's a vampire. Whereas, if the Pope digs one up, they think it's a saint. Idiots!" Ted poked his finger into Bob's chest. "Wait, tell me this: What would a priest in Eastern Orthodoxy think Bob?"

"I don't know."

"He'd think the uncorrupted body was some poor SOB who died under the curse of excommunication by some other priest. That's what! Bob, you don't know your Ba, Ka, Ib, or your Ren from your Sheut. You don't know Sheut! That's funny, isn't it?"

Bob looked to the bathroom door.

"Oh, stop. The attendant is just outside the door, and he'll tell people what I told him; to use another bathroom because this one is under repair. This is hypnosis like you never thought existed. I have that kind of power Bob. But, hell, you're the clever one, so tell me what happens next," he said with a forced coolness burying a simmering anger. "In your *novel* that is."

"Oh that story," Bob said. He struggled to move but could not. Sweat formed on his upper lip, and he spoke with a forced nonchalance. "It was simply a bit of comic relief I indulged myself in. You see, after the failed ceremony, once the sun comes up the next morning, our anti-hero Cedrick wakes up naked in the morgue, complete with toe tag. Then, not realizing that the ritual has actually worked he decides to wait until night to escape from the morgue. But he doesn't know that spell has been reversed for him in one important aspect. See, he's dead by night and alive by day. So, when night falls, he becomes inanimate and wakes up the next morning in the same drawer in the same morgue. Slow learner, that Cedrick."

Ted hit Bob full force with the back of his hand. It caught Bob partially on the nose.

"Bastard!" said Ted. "Real funny for someone minutes from their own demise."

"But you're forgetting one thing. Cedrick."

"What's that? Bob."

"If you kill me, I'll never finish my novel."

Cedrick, nee Ted reddened. He pulled back his hand to strike Bob again but he stopped and simply laughed. "Oh, God! You're simply out of your mind aren't you?" He reached into a side pocket of his khaki shorts and took out what seemed to be an inexpensive disposable pen. However, when he twisted the end, fibers splayed out from one end like a frayed paintbrush. He shook it out and it fluffed out like some dense bloom of a gray-green flower, about two inches in diameter. He held it in front of Bob's eyes. "This should interest you, Bob. It's made from a rare sea creature, a type of tube worm found by volcanic vents, able to latch onto and suck the fluids out of any creature unlucky enough to wander within reach. Let me demonstrate."

Cedrick pulled Bob's unresisting arm forward, twisting it to show the pale side of his wrists. Blue veins throbbed with blood. He applied the device as one might daub paint, but rather than supplying color, it drew it in, a deep red soaked the thousand fine hairs of the brush-like object and soon the main barrel was filling, and then the blood poured out of the end in a fount and splattered noisily on to the tile floor.

"That's enough of that for now," said Cedrick, removing the brush end as a gecko might remove a foot from a wall.

Bob winced from the stinging pain.

Cedrick licked a drop of blood that was hanging from the end of the device and then sucked it dry. "Your blood sugar is a little high. If you were going to live, I'd suggest a checkup." He looked at his watch. "Your death—not mine—will occur in exactly five minutes. Some of your notions are absurd, but others could not be known without inside knowledge, and I expect a concise explanation, within your remaining five minutes, that will lead me to the traitor." Then, checking his watch once again he said, almost to himself, "I have a car waiting, I have time."

"Explanation?" said Bob. "All right. Ten years ago, my youngest sister and her fiancée were vacationing on the Greek island of Santorini. They had moored a rented boat and my sister, not feeling like taking the launch into town for lunch, stayed on the boat to sunbathe. When the others returned, she wasn't there. Hours later, her body was found, drowned."

"Yes? So?"

"I never liked Bruce, her intended, nor his friends. I suspected... I don't know what. I demanded an autopsy. There were no drugs but also no red blood cells. The physician performing the autopsy asked me if my sister had been suffering from Leukemia. She had not. I suspected foul play, naturally, but the only mark upon her was a large bruise on her thigh. The police suspected it was caused by tripping over the railing. He looked down at his inflamed wrist. "But now I finally know."

"How could *that* possibly lead you to me? Your knowledge of my condition; it can't be coincidence. You sought me out to confront me. You had to know it would be suicide. But how did you find me?"

"I began by looking into other strange deaths. I am seriously wealthy. I didn't lie about that. And there is a virtual army of poor yet well-qualified graduate students of a variety of disciplines throughout the world. I quickly put together somewhat of a world-wide epidemiological map of strange deaths, where the cause was either lack of blood or where lack of blood was suspected in causing a fatal accident; perhaps lack of blood due to unknown sudden onset of Leukemia. I also sought out stories of wrongfully diagnosed deaths, where supposed corpses revived, perhaps even on the autopsy table. Because, no matter how careful, a vampire will, at times, misjudge time of day. War zones are a frequent and convenient venue for the vampire—they may not make it to a safe haven and be found, as a seeming corpse only to disappear later. With you, it was in some ways easier to correlate stories. You are unique: Alive by day, and a corpse by night."

"Oh, I remember now! Not your sister of course, but Santorini and then the other islands. You can't imagine how those jet skis, changed my life. You can't imagine. I confer with my fellows, of course, in writing, due to our *conflicting schedules*, I tell them how easy they have it compared to me. To hunt under the cover of darkness is one thing, but quite another to find sustenance in the broad daylight—to put food on the table as you so quaintly put it."

Bob had a disturbing mental image of someone actually laying on a kitchen table, perhaps in Wisconsin, watching in hypnogogic horror as the previously unassuming Ted, or whatever name he used that day, slowly drained them of their blood.

"But I ask you, who else could have thrived? What is Richard's line? *And I nothing to back my suit at all, But the plain devil and dissembling looks.* Well, don't I have that same boast; against all odds?" Cedrick seemed lost in thought for a second. "But, the jet skis, yes, to drive right up, food lying out, usually asleep, half naked, greased and ready on the slippery fiberglass bow, just ready for you to stand up on your mount and pull your prey into the water and consume them in the shadow of the hull. What an innovation. Then, no disposal problems, you just leave them floating, another unfortunate drowning."

Bob quaked within his body, frozen under the hypnotic spell.

"Oh, Bob, you want to kill me, ho hum, I know. However, you have mere minutes to tell me how clever you've been, sussing out vampire lore and legend and how you know such exacting details that only a handful know."

"It's amazing what an addict will do for a fix."

"You're not making any sense."

"We made a prisoner of one of your little chums and he ratted you out. Is that clear enough for you?"

"We?"

"Yes, we," Bob said. He looked and felt odd, splayed flat against the tile wall; immobile except for his head. "I soon found I wasn't alone in my little vampire hunting expedition. It's a small fraternity, and eventually you bump up against each other without even trying. But if you mourned the loss of your good pal Vincent, the rumors of his demise are highly exaggerated."

"Vincent wouldn't talk."

Bob laughed. "He would, he has, he will. He's in a sort of jail."

"Locked up? You have no right. You can't create magic, you can't understand magic, yet you seem to have an uncanny ability to debase it. But now that you've told me, surely you know I'll rescue him. Is that your stupid plan? Use Vincent as a lure with you bravely sacrificing your life. Idiots! You will die and your friends will die. Frankly, I'm starting to enjoy killing your type. The more I see of humans; the more I'm angry about every encroachment of your science upon the realm of magic. The moon! Have you no shame? To tread upon a goddess? What evil vanity. Who gave you the right?" He held the blood wand high.

Cedrick put the blood wand away. "Oh, what the hell, let's do it the old fashioned way, just for old time's sake." He bared his teeth, grabbing Bob by the hair, an unresisting head tilted, exposing the jugular vein, pulsing under the pressure of fear. And then Cedrick moved in, quickly at first but then, like Zeno's paradox, he covered half the distance in the blink of an eye, and half the next a bit slower, and finally Cedrick's fleshy head stiffened and froze in place as though fashioned from quick setting gel.

Bob let out a breath and Cedrick's unconscious body slid down his and on to the tile floor. Bob found that limbs moved of his own volition once more. He retrieved an object that he had tucked into his back waistband and stood over the body of his attacker.

"For Elise," he said as tears of rage filled his eyes.

• • •

"You make the sale?" the bartender asked.

"Yes, the extra ten minutes was a life saver," Bob's hand was trembling as he handed the bartender a stack of bills amounting to two hundred Singapore dollars. "My additional appreciation for helping me."

"Wow, two hundred more," said the bartender, counting the bills. "I felt pretty bad fooling him about the time, but only ten minutes, right?"

"Sure, what harm could come from that. What time have you?"

The bartender pulled out a cell phone from his pants pocket and looked at it. "Seven twenty-eight."

"Sunset was at seven-fourteen," Bob Smith declared.

"Here, it always is boss, there about. Every day. That old sun, rolling over his planet, taking stock, seeing what us little ants are doing all day. And then he goes to bed, just like my little boy, tucked in for the night. The greater light goes to bed, and the lesser light takes over, and the stars are in the firmament, that's in your Bible."

"And your Buddha, what did he say?"

"I follow Confucianism, but the Buddha, he says..."

The bartender stopped. He was staring over Bob's shoulder. "Hey, there's a bunch of people over by the can. Looks like something happened. That's the hotel medic."

"Let's hope it's nothing serious," Bob said, turning to look.

"Yeah, one time, I'm on my shift and a guy had a heart attack, taking a crap, the found him sitting on the john. No tip for Jimmy."

"Thanks, Jimmy." Bob said and walked away. He got a few paces and turned. "So, what did the Buddha say?"

Jimmy called after him, "Buddha say, The Way is not in the stars."

"Nor the moon." Bob gave a half nod, half salute, turned and walked away.

After watching the commotion at the bathrooms and the removal of a stretcher, Jimmy proceeded to clean up the plates. Under one of the fine linen napkins, where his high tipping customer had just been standing and chatting, a spot of red was growing on the fine white cloth. He lifted a corner of the napkin gingerly, and underneath a he saw something out of place, something more at home in a museum. He set down the napkin, then lifted it up again quickly. It was still there. He had hoped it would not be. It was a flint knife bound with sinew into an antler horn handle etched with runic symbols and dark with the grime of ages and more, with fresh blood.

Killing Time

Detective Lieutenant Zadroga stared at the gun in the plastic bag that the smirking Sergeant had dropped with a clunk upon Zadroga's cherished wooden desk. He looked up and saw that the Sergeant's other massive paw grasped a shirt collar, hanging from which was a man. Lieutenant Zadroga looked up at the suspect. He seemed a nervous little man; his pale hands entangled and unentangled with a desperation that left alternating red and white indentations on the flesh of his bony fingers. His thinning long hair was mussed, and his short-sleeved, white cotton dress shirt was pulled halfway off one shoulder, the top button missing.

"Think you'll be okay with this desperado?" asked the Sergeant.

Detective Tim Zadroga, nicknamed "Zag," was twenty years with the Greater Boston Police Force. He pursed his lips to stifle a smile. He didn't approve of the Sergeant's tone or treatment of the suspect and didn't want to give the Sergeant the pleasure of seeing his sarcasm pay off.

"Get back to your post, Sergeant," was all that the detective said. The Sergeant's post was the metal detector in the busy lobby, and Zadroga imagined a line was backing up already.

"Right." The Sergeant, clearly unhappy, shrugged and left.

As soon as he closed the office door, the strange little man began to speak. "He tried to accuse me of smuggling in that gun." He jerked his head toward the gun on the desk, unwilling to unclasp his hands. "But as I told him, I tried to get his attention, but he was on the other side of the metal detector, so I just held it out in front of me."

"Then all hell broke loose," said the weary detective, who was all too familiar with that Sergeant's penchant for bullying. This was getting old—this job, this life. He looked at the bizarre energetic little man in front of him. He doubtless had a story to go along with the gun, maybe a rational one for once. Zadroga could only hope.

In the old days, now would be the time when he'd offer the poor man a cigarette. It didn't even matter that he'd finally quit smoking; she had still left him, moving out the last of her belongings just this morning. There was nothing rational about his own story: she, the wife, unhappy all those years for reasons unarticulated, and the daughter, the recent graduate newly employed at a beginning salary greater than his after thirty years. All nests emptied, all debts paid, all obligations met—and the love of his life had simply left him.

"Yes! Hell did break loose. For me, anyway." The little man rubbed his shoulder. "I suspect your Sergeant was enjoying himself at my expense. May I sit down?"

"No, you may not," Zadroga didn't say it to be rude. It was an interrogator's habit; liars prepared their stories carefully and anything to put them off track helped to determine the truth. He looked up at the man to gauge his reaction.

The man calmly sat down in the visitor chair on the other side of the desk, as though he'd heard *yes* instead of *no*.

"Thank you, Detective... Zadroga," he said, carefully sounding out the name while reading the name plaque on the desk. "Unusual name—where is it from?"

The detective ignored the question but made a mental note—*space cadet*. He picked up the single sheet of paper that the Sergeant had placed face down on the desk before dropping the gun a distance of two feet onto the wood surface. Zadroga put off examining the gun because it would mean revealing the mark in the desk's finish that he knew must be there. He could see from its black finish and boxy shape that it was a Glock semi-automatic 9mm. Zadroga himself carried the compact Kel-tec P-32, just enough of a gun to meet department regulations. He read the Sergeant's brief handwritten notes on the incident sheet. It was the carbon copy, not the original—how many times did he have to tell those guys?

Zadroga swiveled in his chair to catch more light from the window. It was a gray, cold day, but the late afternoon's meager sunlight added just enough to make the Sergeant's primitive scribbles legible.

"It says here that you came to turn in what you believe to be a gun used in a crime?"

"A crime?" The man leaned forward, clasping the edge of the desk. "Not just a crime—a murder!"

"We consider murder to be a crime here in Boston, Doctor..." Zadroga squinted at the report.

"Doctor Smith. Doctor Roland K. Smith, Massachusetts Institute of Technology, Cambridge. I'm with the Center for Theoretical Physics."

"May I see some ID? Do you have a card?"

Doctor Smith pulled a driver's license from his wallet and handed it to Zadroga, along with a business card. After briefly examining them, tilting the license in the light, Zadroga rose and leaned across the desk to extend his hand, which was accepted.

"Doctor Smith, Detective Zadroga. I'm sorry if you were roughed up a little downstairs, it's their job to be careful."

Smith sat back and smoothed his hopelessly crumpled shirt. "Apology accepted." There was no irony in his voice.

"Off to a rocky start, but that's what we face in science. If we quit whenever thwarted, where would we be?"

"Bashing each other with rocks instead of shooting each other with guns?" quipped Zadroga. He picked up the gun with the corner of the plastic bag and smiled when he could not discern any indentation in his desk. *Thank God for small favors.* "Care to explain? I need to warn you to keep it brief; it's past my nap time and I get bored easily."

"All right then." Smith took a deep breath and spoke quickly. "I murdered my grandfather with that weapon."

• • •

It took a while to move forward again. There was the reading of the rights. Smith waived his right to an attorney and Zadroga taped the remainder of the conversation. The man was in his 50's and it was possible that he had a surviving grandfather—perhaps a mercy killing—it was equally possible that he would hear little more than the ramblings of a loon.

So, when Zadroga's wife called, he picked up. Could he get some copies made of pictures in the photo albums? She didn't want to take them without leaving him copies of the photos. *Great*, he thought, *if she was so unhappy, why would she want the memories?* And then he wondered that same thing about himself. It was hard to accept that she hadn't loved him all those years, but was rather enduring their shared life, waiting for the kid to finish college, waiting until there was finally enough joint wealth. Then *zoom*, no longer a cop's wife. If he could just go back ten years and smack himself awake. He had a chance ten years ago with someone who may have really loved him, and he had chosen the honest path, the good husband. Look where it got him now.

Hitting the record button and stating all the required particulars, Zadroga said, "Start at the beginning."

"The beginning, Detective?" Smith laughed. "Oh, the precious irony; you have no idea."

"I'm starting to think so."

"I'm breaking several laws to tell you this, you know."

"No, Dr. Smith, I don't know. Such is the purpose of you talking and me listening."

"Not your little laws, mind you. Bigger laws!"

Zadroga decided he'd give him one more minute before calling for the squirrels; his name for the nut collectors in the white jackets. He looked at his watch; it was a quarter to five. Newly single, his approaching options were the sports bar or an empty house. He chose to stay a little longer. He prompted Smith. "Bigger laws? Like what? The UN?"

"The UN? Oh, don't be foolish. The laws of nature, of course."

"Oh, God," Zadroga sighed. Brushing his hair back, he leaned forward and opened the bottom drawer of his desk. "You want a drink, Doc? I'm gonna make a call to some nice people who are just dying to talk to you about this. May be your last chance to drink for a long, long time."

"I see," said Smith, studying the detective's face. "You think I'm crazy."

"Doc, ever think of going into psychiatry yourself? Because you see through me like I'm Claude Rains." He unsealed a bottle of single barrel Irish whiskey and poured two fingers in a simple clear glass tumbler.

"Whiskey in the bottom drawer, just like the detectives in the movies!" Smith exclaimed, his eyes lighting up like a schoolboy's.

"Except this ain't no apple juice, Doc. And you're thinking of Sam Spade, not Boston's finest." Zadroga knocked back a satisfying mouthful. He'd never had a drink on duty before. The whiskey had been a gift to him upon his daughter landing *her* job. He supposed there was a note of independence in that gesture, telling the old man that, now, she could afford an expensive gift. She made him promise he'd keep it in his bottom desk drawer, just like the movie detectives—cute kid. He picked up the phone and started to dial.

"All right, all right, Detective. It started at the lab. There was an argument."

Zadroga put down the phone and smiled. "That's better. An argument with your grandfather. He must be in his nineties because you look fifty."

"Fifty-five actually; nature has been kind. Or, perhaps the days confined to the lab, and the avoidance of skin-aging UV rays."

"Fifty-five, dad seventy-five maybe, grandfather was ninety-five?" asked Zadroga, counting on his fingers.

"No, he's dead."

"Yeah, you said you killed him. That's why we're having this little chat."

"I can see where that line of thinking will lead, and to avoid being accused of being obtuse or insane, let me clarify at this point. I mean simply that the argument of which I speak was not with my grandfather, but rather, with a group of fellow scientists. I have no animosity whatsoever toward my grandfather. In fact, I did not know him."

"Not again." Zadroga slumped in his chair.

"I understand your frustration, Detective, but if you will let me continue, this is about a dispute that I'm having with my fellow physicists. Moreover, you shall be the arbitrator of said dispute. Those fools in my department pushed me to this point." He trailed off and lifted his hand in a gesture of helplessness.

"Where you murdered your grandfather?"

"Precisely."

"If I had more than a cat to go home to, you'd be telling this to the guys in white coats right now. But as for now, Doc, you've got to be more entertaining than whatever's waiting in my mailbox from Netflix. So, please," Zadroga said. He planted his feet on the part of the desk that was covered with a felt-backed writing pad and gestured with his glass. "Continue."

Continue Doctor Smith did, and over the next half hour, he explained the secret research his lab was involved in. It was *time travel*. And that was firmly among topics Zadroga wouldn't have been surprised at when dealing with any nut case. But Zadroga knew that a real gun in the hands of a real crazy person could easily have a real crime behind it. While the story could be a crock, some metaphorical version would uncover a tragic and all too real truth. So he played along.

"Hodes! He made me so angry." Smith continued.

"Doctor Hodes, the third leg of your time travel trio; the parallel ten dimensions guy?"

"Yes! The fool! Well, not as much of a fool as Jawahar, I grant him that, but still deeply opposed to pre-interference. Why? If it did prove impossible to interfere with our own timeline, why not improve life for someone, even if in another parallel universe? What could be the harm?"

"Seems harmless to me," said Zadroga, now feeling more than an insignificant effect after two large glasses of whiskey and dizzy from the lecture about possible futures and time paradoxes. But the lump in his chest was gone, and he felt thankful for that. He was reassessing his strict two-beer limit, no hard liquor rule. While they were talking, Zadroga had also Googled the doctor on his PC, and the topics of papers by Smith and the other two he'd mentioned—Hodes, and Jawahar—did skirt what one might consider the concept of violating time.

"Harmless or not," continued Smith, "it's our duty. It's as if a surgeon has a scalpel and refuses to use it because it may leave a scar!"

"A scar in time?"

"Precisely! A scar in time. That's it exactly. Detective, you are far more clever than you know. If only my fellow colleagues had your intuitive grasp of the issue. Everyone accepts the idea that correcting pathologies creates risk for the patient. Of course, there is a difficult recovery period. Of course, there is a residual effect, or a scar, if you like. Yes, I like that. A scar in time." He paused, staring unfocused, as if at a point beyond the room, then said, "I think I will have that drink now, if you don't mind, Detective."

Zadroga fished another tumbler from his desk drawer with two fingers and poured about four ounces. "Sorry, no ice." He handed it to Smith, who sniffed it carefully before taking a small sip.

"Thank you. It's very good," he commented. "The tannins are surprisingly well polymerized for this type of whiskey. I'd say, over ten years in oak barrels. Am I right?"

"What?" Zadroga was taken aback. "Let's see." He turned the bottle in his hand; it said Redbreast, Irish Whiskey. "What do you know, twelve years old, in oak barrels, single still, whatever the hell that means. My daughter gave me this last St. Paddy's Day. I'm usually having a beer about now, but this is nice. So, what about this time thing? You said that you found a way to curve lasers?"

"The *light* from lasers." Smith held up a warning finger. "Science is about using the correct language."

"Okay, the light from lasers goes into a loop, like a tube, and when you're in it, time works differently. But." he said, interjecting quickly, seeing that Smith was about to correct him again, "it's no ordinary tube because a tube would be open at each end and time would leak in and out. In our dimension, it still looks like a tube, except that in some other dimension it's counter-rotating at ninety degrees making it like. Don't tell me." He struggled for the words. "A multi-dimensional hyper-tube—more like a cocoon of light."

"Yes, very good Detective Zadroga. That was the genius of Jawahar and his theories on multi-dimensional optics, but when actuated, we found that the resulting interference patterns directly mimicked the action of the other six unseen dimensions. That was a surprise to everyone, it actually worked *out of the box*, so to speak. We thought we were only on the threshold, but we found that we had already passed through the gate."

"And this cocoon is large enough for someone to sit inside."

"Yes, yes. Not intentionally, mind you, but certain non-miniaturized components were less expensive, just making due with meager funds. Of course, we didn't consider putting anyone inside. We had other means to assess our progress—atomic clocks, precisely decaying isotopes, and such."

"Didn't bother to tell someone? The government for example?"

"The government? Oh please. Yes, we told them enough to keep our funding, but understated our progress. The three of us. Me, Hodes, and Jawahar. We knew we could trust no one with what could be the ultimate power."

"To change the past?"

"Yes, sadly, only the past. As I said, we don't have future travel figured out yet, although I feel that is only a matter of time, maybe five, maybe ten years."

"When you figure it out, why not go in the future and tell yourself to come back here and tell yourself? You'd save a lot of time, wouldn't you?"

"Oh, Detective, there you have it," said Smith, not sensing in the least Zadroga's sarcasm. "But it is the past where we can improve the present. Think about going back to a rudimentary apothecary in the Middle Ages and giving them the knowledge to make penicillin in time to prevent the plague. What of that?"

"Wouldn't that change the present? I mean in some way where you didn't even discover this time machine?"

"Or didn't exist at all? That was the nature of our dispute. We were three rams with locked horns. It was all due to Hodes ridiculous citation of an idea by a science fiction writer. The paradox wherein time travel could not exist because if it did, one could travel back in time, kill one's own grandfather, thus one's father's father."

"I think I know what a grandfather is."

Smith tittered. "Heh, of course. But seriously, thus, progenitor expired, a progeny—you—no more! Or so the so-called Grandfather paradox predicts."

"So you shot your grandfather. Makes perfect sense." It was getting on six o'clock and his stomach was starting to complain. It was time to get the flat statement of fact, get this gun down to the lab, get a paraffin test on the good doctor and lock him up, at least for tonight. "Doctor, fun time's over. One, did you fire this gun within the last twenty-four hours? Yes, or no? I need suspicion before I order tests, they're expensive."

"I don't know how to answer that!"

"You can't *not* know how to answer such a stupid fucking simple question!" Zadroga pounded the side of his fist into the desk, and several objects toppled in the minor quake. Pens rolled onto the linoleum floor with a clatter. A good cop had to know how to use anger effectively when interviewing suspects, but Zadroga found himself trembling after this display. He tensed to control himself, as though if he didn't, something bottled up inside him would escape; a dam break.

"Yes." Dr. Smith stuttered a bit, rattled by Zadroga's display of temper. "Yes is the most useful reply, as far as your paraffin test is concerned."

"Good," said Zadroga. "Now, did you, as you stated before, use this gun to shoot someone? Someone you believed died as a result of that shooting?"

"Yes."

"Yes. Just plain yes?"

"Yes."

Zadroga eyed him suspiciously. "Where's the body?"

"Buried. I have the address." Smith took a folded piece of paper from his right front pants pocket and handed it to Zadroga. "Can we proceed with both the paraffin and the ballistics tests now?"

Zadroga unfolded the paper. He didn't recognize the address but it looked to be not far from the station, perhaps why Smith had chosen him, or at least this station. It was now a little too real. This little man, whom Zadroga had come to like in some strange way in the past hour, as one might some autistic and innocent child, was really starting to look as though he were a murderer.

• • •

Zebedee Smith: Born 1902, Died 1931.

Detective Zadroga stared at the headstone and laughed. The address turned out to be a small grave yard surrounded by a residential neighborhood and Smith had led him to this particular plot. Zadroga had been skeptical of the scientist's claims, and perhaps more so of the murder than the time-travel because Dr. Smith just didn't seem to have a malicious bone in his body, so to have killed his ninety-five year old grandfather was unthinkable. However, the paraffin test had come up positive, and the gun had been fired recently. They fired a round to have a bullet to have to compare, but now he was looking at a grave that had clearly been undisturbed for decades.

Dr. Smith had been adamant about the exhumation and murder or not, he was the only surviving relative. The paperwork was filed, and denied. Anyone could simply look at the moss and patina on the slab-covered gravesite to tell that it had lain undisturbed for a very, very long time. He pointed out the undisturbed nature of the grave to Smith.

"But that isn't the point!" a red-faced Smith said. He pulled Zadroga aside. "Everything we discussed! I gave you classified information. You must believe me. Look at the date! 1931! It was before my own father was conceived. Can't you see? I did it? I killed my own grandfather, and yet I live! It is a scar in time. The very fabric of reality is askew, yet we still exist. The Universe could care less if we have a Grandfather Paradox."

"Unless you've got a bottle of champagne to pop, to go along with that speech, I think we're done here," said Zadroga.

Zadroga had thought it would be worthwhile to see where Smith claimed a body might be buried but he was apparently wrong. He had discussed Smith with the staff psychologist, Riki Lindhome. She had a slight concern that someone—a representative victim for the grandfather in the time-travel delusion—may have been murdered by Smith. Zadroga didn't see Smith for a murderer, but Smith could have been so overwrought and fixated that he had actually carried out his delusion, symbolically. Lindehome recommended involuntary commitment for observation. And Lindhome's concerns now meant that all known acquaintances of Smith should probably be accounted for. That necessitated interviews with Smith's colleagues, Hodes, and Jawahar.

• • •

"He told you?" Hodes blurted out before thinking. He was obviously not someone used to employing deception. "I mean, he said what?"

"Time travel," said the detective. They had met for breakfast at an IHOP restaurant and now sat in a sunlit booth with a scenic view consisting of the hood of a blue Dodge Durango. Hodes had insisted on meeting off campus for breakfast, across the Charles River from MIT. Hodes studied the menu for a long time before finally ordering the International Crepes. The detective ordered three eggs, over easy, and pancakes.

Hodes was an exceptionally tall, horse-faced man; deep vertical lines in his deeply browned face seemed to pull down at the corners of his eyes. Zadroga guessed he was in his mid-sixties and while far from fat, his thin arms and thickish midsection gave the appearance that he hadn't exercised anything but his brain in at least twenty years.

"Time travel," Hodes repeated, enunciating clearly between a bite of crepe. "He said that?"

Zadroga didn't reply. This was the second or third go-around on the same topic. He'd just leave Hodes in silence and see how the other man filled it in.

Hodes fidgeted, before finally cracking. "Not to make fun, after all he is currently under psychiatric care, but when he had this time travel fantasy, did he happen to say what he might have done by any chance?"

"Yes."

The abrupt answer seemed to startle Hodes. "Did he? Oh my. Because we, the three of us, had so many speculative conversations; all blue sky and kid's play. Musings to be succinct"

"In those musing, did Smith happen to mentioned suicide?"

"Suicide?"

"Yes. Apparently when the doctor on staff at Belleview contacted the list of people Smith gave as references, someone, or maybe all of them, claimed that Smith had threatened to kill himself. I have to think that you and Jawahar were contacted. Suicide triggers a whole string of events in an institution like that. Makes him a danger to himself, removes general liberty, and isolates Smith. Pretty clever way to shut him up, if that was the intent."

"I'm sure I don't know what you mean."

"Ever hear Smith talk about suicide? Did you talk to his doctors?"

"I'm sure that if I did, I would respect his privacy," Hodes said firmly.

"I see. Okay, then, let's talk about the effect of changing past events. Not that I believe it, but I understand that Smith was all for it."

"For it?" Hodes almost choked on a strawberry. He reached for his water and drank half the glass before taking it away from his lips.

"I'm not the enemy, Hodes. I'm just a cop. I don't know what you boffins have been up to, and I'm not sure I care, but you've done nothing but make me more suspicious. I'm going to lay my cards on the table all the same; maybe not the best metaphor at an IHOP, with all this pancake syrup."

Hodes laughed. Usually a good sign someone was disarmed and likely to be honest.

"So here's the problem," began Zadroga. "Your buddy Smith showed up with a gun and a crazy story. The gun had been fired recently, and paraffin tests showed that Smith had fired a gun. Crazy guy... gun... claims that he shot someone. With me?"

"Yes, I see the need for concern."

"Here's where it gets tricky. He says he shot someone, but to make a long story short, it was someone that he couldn't have shot. But we—we being me and the staff psychologist--wonder if he shot someone else, thinking in his fevered brain somewhere it was the other guy. Follow? What Freud would call transference, or was that projection?"

"I wouldn't know psychiatry terms; I'm a scientist. But I follow what you're saying."

"So, I'm naturally concerned that he was so deep into his delusion—perhaps some temporary psychosis stemming from overwork—that he may have actually shot somebody."

Hodes had stopped eating and was gazing down at his plate, the tines of his fork tracing patterns in the blueberry syrup. Zadroga watched the lines slowly filled in again, unlike real scars, like the jagged knife wound too close to his heart, the tense days wondering whether the damaged liver would heal, the excuses she made for not visiting him in the hospital, the aversion she felt toward the topic, or toward the mere sight of his healed flesh, even years later. It was shortly after that when he had met Julie.

Hodes' fork slipped and clattered across the table.

Zadroga picked up the fork with a napkin and handed it back to Hodes.

"Thank you Detective. Smith didn't happen to mention who he killed, did he? I mean, just in case it *is* someone that perhaps Jawahar or I might recognize it as a likely symbolic substitution. It is a university and people come and go but maybe there are acquaintances we should check up on."

"His grandfather. On his father's side."

"Oh, no. This could be bad."

"Don't worry, couldn't have happened. His grandfather died in 1931, according to his tombstone. Do you have someone in mind who might symbolically substitute for the grandfather?"

"This could be very, very bad," Hodes mused aloud, staring out the window at nothing in particular.

"Dr. Hodes," said Zadroga sharply.

"Very bad," he repeated, dropping his fork again.

Detective Zadroga flagged down the waitress for the check. He was beginning to suspect that all that the three scientists had managed to invent was simply a do-it-yourself crazy kit.

• • •

At 6 p.m., they assembled at Dr. Hodes' house. Zadroga, Hodes, and Jawahar stood in the kitchen of the modest two-story craftsman house just off the MIT campus in Cambridgeport. Hodes was a bachelor, like Smith. He had started coffee and was trying to locate corn chips or some other snacks that he thought might exist deep in a cupboard.

"I agree, Detective Zadroga," said Hodes. "I agree insofar as Smith hasn't a malicious bone in his body. The problem is, as I see it, he hasn't a compassionate one either."

"There was that problem with the grad assistants," said Jawahar in his Indian accent. "Do you remember?"

"Oh, *that*," Hodes said. "The cell phone radiation experiments. No harm done."

"Oh no?" Jawahar said, stepping in to confront the much taller Hodes. He jabbed at Hodes' chest, seemingly trying to break a rib. "It was an abuse of power. Experimenting upon the poor students, and the animals—those rabbits, he had no sign-off, what-is-that-thing, for those as well. You must admit!"

"Ow!" Hodes, shielded his sternum with a large hand. "Okay, okay, you win."

"That's right," said Dr. Jawahar triumphantly. "And another thing, I tell you all." His pointed finger circled the group. "The cat is out of the bag. What is done is done. Smith is locked away, and he cannot get to the machine, but we need to know what has been done. We are having this detective who has been sent, and that is our only hope for getting at the truth. Or you two can go and jump in a lake."

• • •

They went on to confirm what Smith had described of their experiments. What Zadroga provided was details, names and dates from the story Smith had told him.

Hodes summed it up. "We're used to our lab containing the experimental parameters, and now we must look to the world, humanity, and perhaps the universe itself for evidence of Smith's—one man's—experiment. Sort of turns things on its head, doesn't it?"

"How's that?" said Zadroga.

"Before, we were but men trying to figure out what the universe had done. Perhaps now the universe is wondering how to cope with the actions of a single man?"

There was a brief silence, as everyone paused to consider those words.

Then Jawahar, suddenly threw his hands up. "So that's one small step for Smith, one cataclysmic end to space-time for the rest of us? I can't accept that. Listen to what you are saying."

The detective cleared his throat. He hated to even pretend to contribute, but he wanted to mention something Smith had said about the scar in time. But, *oh for God's sake*, he suddenly realized, these egg heads were not just out on a limb but *out on a limb on a limb!*

"I hate to forestall the end of the world gentlemen," he said. "But we're in serious danger of being totally full of shit, pardon my French, because we haven't verified one damn thing Smith has claimed."

"We know the device works," said Hodes.

"So?" replied Zadroga. "Did anyone see Smith using it?"

"He must have snuck in," offered Hodes. "Because we know it was used from the computer logs."

"Circumstantial.," said Zadroga. "Prove it to me. Smith traveled back to 1931 and shot Zebedee Smith."

"Ballistics?" asked Jawahar.

"Dr. Jawahar, with all due respect, it'd be us digging up Zebedee Smith in the dead of night, because I can tell you that no official will approve a disinterment based on these grounds. I personally don't feel like ending my career by carving out a bullet from some desiccated carcass; said bullet most likely removed in the autopsy at the time. That's if the old guy was shot at all, which I doubt. And then we'd have to get the bullet examined at a police lab, with no paperwork from the prosecutor's office whatsoever authorizing the lab to compare this bullet, which may or may not exist, with the test slug I got yesterday, hinging on the story from the lips of a man who, may I remind you, is now in a rubber room at Belleview?"

"Actually, you have our testimony also." Jawahar said.

Zadroga smacked himself on the forehead.

"If I may," said Jawahar. He rose from the kitchen stool where he was seated. "A compromise, perhaps? Let's look into some basic facts. Smith's claim is that he has changed history. His claim is that his father was born in 1932, whereas his father's father died in 1931. Can we see if we can locate online genealogical records? Hodes?"

"Oh, right, ask the ex-Mormon," Hodes said.

"Granted, ex-Mormon. Well?"

"I do have an account for several genealogical research sites," Hodes said. "A hard habit to break."

• • •

"Of course I'm sure," insisted Hodes. "I learned this at my mother's knee. Besides, *Zebedee* Smith?"

"So?" said Jawahar.

"Unusual Western name," Hodes pointed out, without missing a beat. "And I can follow his WWI service records. It is the same man."

They had retired to Hodes' office, set up in a spare first floor bedroom, and were all standing hunched over to better see. The glow from a flat screen monitor was the primary light in the dim room. One small window was blocked by an overgrown laurel, the only thing visible through the dingy panes of unwashed glass.

"Yet," said Jawahar, "this one website says that he died in 1931, and this other that he died just eight years ago. And all the others, the link is broken when you click on his name."

"Hell," said Zadroga, "if he did live recently, I can track him through public records. Let me at that thing."

The detective exchanged seats with Jawahar and signed on to various city and state resources that he had passwords for: licensing, tickets and arrest records, and city taxes. It seemed that here too, Zebedee Smith both existed and did not exist, receiving a parking ticket in 1993, but the recorded driver's license number, although listed on the Secretary of State's records, returned only an error message for a broken link. The death certificate confirmed the tombstone date of 1931, but a marriage license for his second marriage after the death of his first wife was marked 1975.

"We need to talk to Smith," Zadroga said. "All of us."

"But he is locked up!" said Jawahar.

"You all saw to that," retorted Zadroga. He watched Hodes look away and lower his head. "Don't worry; I'll take care of it."

"I know," said Jawahar, conspiratorially. "You will call in some favors."

Zadroga laughed. "The police department that I live in works on forms, not favors. Everyone wants written proof that it won't be their ass in a sling when things go tits up. It would be good if the three of you can meet me at the hospital tomorrow. I'll get a release based on a supervised visit to a suspected crime scene."

"What crime scene?" Jawahar asked.

"The one on the Moon, my friend," said Hodes, clasping Jawahar by the upper arm. "Or hopefully a good restaurant."

• • •

"You told them I was suicidal?" Smith was hopping mad; actually hopping with every other word in his seat in the restaurant booth. There were the four of them, with Zadroga sitting in a chair that was brought to the end of the table. "There were insane people there—I had to be in the same room as them! Do you know what that's like?"

"We're all starting to get an idea," said Zadroga. Hodes and Jawahar stifled snickers, and Zadroga waited for another rant from Smith to begin.

Instead, Smith stared past Zadroga; their waitress had shown up.

"Excuse me, can I start you gentlemen off with something from the bar, or are you ready to order?"

She was young, with pale skin black shiny hair, pulled back in a ponytail. Her bangs partially hid large green eyes. A smile on lips painted blood red revealed straight teeth, but for one crooked incisor. At first, Zadroga thought *Goth*, but when she spoke he realized she must be an Eastern Bloc immigrant. The scientists suddenly became as stunned as darted rhinos on a National Geographic special. Zadroga imagined them all, heads buried in textbooks through puberty until this moment. Did they never get out of the lab?

She took their orders; a process extended by various show-off questions concerning menu items.

When she left, Zadroga clapped his hands twice. "Getting to the matter at hand, Doctor Smith, what proof have you that you traveled back in time and shot Zebedee Smith in 1931?"

"The ballistics should show that," he answered confidently.

"I have that bullet from the gun you gave me. What do we compare it to?"

"The bullet in Zebedee." Smith's tone all but said, *you fool*.

"And Zebedee is where?"

"Waiting to be dug up?"

"By whose authority?"

"Oh," said Smith. "I see."

The detective waited until everyone was silent for a minute before reaching into his coat pocket and then placing a small cardboard box upon the table. It was oblong, perhaps something that would fit in a particular type of storage cabinet.

"Did you gentlemen know that the first case involving forensic ballistics was in 1918, in Albany, New York? That being the study of the microscopic examination of the grooves left on the soft lead of a bullet by a particular gun."

"And this," said Hodes, pointing at the box with his steak knife. "Can we assume, due to the theatrics that this may be the bullet, removed from the corpse of the murdered Zebedee Smith in 1931, taken during an autopsy at that time."

"Yes," said Detective Zadroga. "I left early this morning and," he nodded to Jawahar. "I called in some favors."

"But the criminal justice system runs on paper, you said."

"As does NYU's Museum of Forensic Science but I have a cousin who teaches there, and he contacted the professor who acts as curator."

"Why a museum?" asked Hodes.

"Who cares, you fool!" said Smith. "Detective, tell them how it compares to the bullet from the gun I gave you."

"Let's take Hodes's question first," said Zadroga. "I went to the museum for two reasons. One: Zebedee Smith was a Judge in the Circuit Court, and one Guido Spetzicoli, an anarchist, was found guilty of the crime. The crime was sensational at the time because it was assumed to be the act of an anarchist. Anarchists were the Muslim terrorists of the day. And two, because the ballistic investigation could not tie the bullet to any known weapon of its time. Spetzicoli was convicted, despite the fact that the murder weapon was never found.

Zadroga stared purposely at Smith. "All *known* matters relating to that miscarriage of justice are available for study in the Forensics Museum which is an adjunct to the NYU law school."

"Oh, and a third thing—how could I forget?" He opened the lid on the box. Then he lifted a flat piece of cotton padding. Sitting underneath was a brass bullet cartridge. "This was found at the crime scene. A cartridge is ejected from a semi-automatic when it fires. It mystified the investigators, because although the automatic pistol was in use at the time, it was rare, and this cartridge could not be identified."

Jawahar turned to Smith "You really killed your grandfather? How could you?"

"It is a rather monstrous act," said Hodes, "you must admit."

"But, but," Smith sputtered. "You still don't get it! If you hadn't conspired to lock me up, it would have all been over by now. I've only killed him until I can set it right again—well part right as it turns out—but only that long. I had to prove a point."

"But Novikov!" Hodes said.

"Novikov is horseshit," Smith retorted.

"Excuse me?" Zadroga. "Non-scientist in the room."

Hodes sighed and then said, "The Novikov self-consistency principle. Briefly, if any action precipitates a paradox, it must be impossible. Therefore what we call, *The Grandfather Paradox*. That is the principle which our friend Dr. Smith was so adamant to disprove. At great risk to the entire space-time continuum, I might add."

"Horseshit and double horseshit!" Smith said. He slammed an open hand on the table. "Any thousands of black holes, right now, are tearing the crap out of your precious space-time. Wait!" He pointed upwards. "There goes another paradox! What the blazes are three little humans, just evolved out of the monkey farm, going to do with our silly little laser beams that isn't happening out there, some place, on a much more massive scale already? Huh? Answer me that!"

"You broke the links on the official LDS ancestor research web page." said Hodes. "That's serious."

They all looked slack-jawed at Hodes.

Zadroga took a bite of his pasta and felt his stomach with his hand. Every time he ate, he thought of the portion of his colon that needed sewing back together after the attack. *It was the quiet ones that you had to watch out for.* This one had been a jumper on a freeway overpass, armed with a *shoto* knife, a souvenir from his father's WWII service. Zadroga become the CIA agent who had been beaming messages into his head. Zadroga was never convinced that the surgeons got the two sides quite matched up because he often felt a random stabbing pain after a large meal.

There was another bad memory he associated with eating. It had occurred one evening, shortly after the attack. He'd been home on leave due to the injury and, at the time, had chalked it up to the fact that he'd been in her hair because she had to take care of him; anyone might say something regrettable. Now he knew, it wasn't a weak moment, but rather a truth long suppressed. He was eating ice cream after dinner one night when she said, in a voice so bitter he hardly recognized it as hers, "Sometimes I just can't stand to watch you eat!"

"A scar, Dr. Smith," Zadroga said aloud. "Like we talked about before, a scar in time."

"Yes!" beamed Smith. "Our memories, our precious human records, may be out of synch, like a room split apart by an earthquake, or phone lines separated by a falling tree. But space-time doesn't care. Space-time doesn't care that our silly memories, whether up here." He tapped his head. "...or on our Web pages, or in our history books make sense, as if they did in the first place."

"I think we'd have noticed," Hodes said. He spoke to Zadroga, "The assumption is that if, at any point in the future, time travel to the past is possible, it would already have happened."

"That make sense."

"Of course it does. If someone in the future can go to the past, we're in the past, so we would have seen the effect." He pulled a pipe from his jacket pocket and clamped it between his teeth. He may as well as said Q.E.D.

Smith broke in. "You don't see evidence of meddling from the future? Tell me Detective, what's the first thing someone might do?"

"With a time machine? I don't know, save JFK? Or at least settle who shot him."

"See!" Smith said. A bit of spittle formed on his lower lip.

"According to you, it would create a paradox, no a wound or fracture where..."

"More than one..." Smith said, helping.

"Versions exist."

"But branching," Jawahar said.

"Not branching, creating complexity, complexity for our little monkey brains. We have to accept reality. Not branching; complexity. Complexity for our confused little monkey brains. We have to accept reality. That assassination took place in front of well over a thousand witnesses and how many credible versions are there? Even the bullets are here or there and then on a hospital gurney. It would be one of the major past sites for people trying to fix things in the past. It fits observation."

"No, no, no," Hodes said, waving his arms. "Speculation. Let's get back to your grandfather."

"Yes, the body," Jawahar said.

"The body?" said Smith. "Think of the gravestone as a memory location on a hard drive that records events in 1931. The universe didn't etch that date into that stone, the universe does not read or write, we do. And how is that the same as claiming there is a body in that grave? What if the body of Zebedee Smith lies in his grave in New Jersey dated 2001? What if there is a body in both? Don't you see? We are the only ones concerned with keeping some linear memory intact, not the universe. Even a simple beam of light experiences time differently than us. Tachyons at the subatomic scale travel backward in time. The universe doesn't give a rat's ass if we're confused or not."

Hodes picked up the box, withdrew the dull, slightly misshapen slug of lead and hefted it in his hand. He let it drop to the table, where it made a satisfying thud on the white tablecloth. "My God. What next? I don't know about you, but I need time to think."

• • •

The last time the group fired up the machine was to give Smith the opportunity to un-kill his grandfather. Zadroga watched Smith sit in an ordinary office chair. Hodes wheeled in a sturdy metal frame, its purpose disguised as a simple equipment rack. Jawahar and Hodes attached optical components to fixed locations, labeled with a marking pen. A dedicated laptop was hooked up and booted up. The graphics on the monitor, Jawahar explained, were a clever mash-up of Google Earth and an astronomy program. It was point-and-click time travel.

They all agreed to a year-long moratorium on using the equipment. Smith, who was anxious to immediately start correcting several of what he saw as humanity's past defects, attempted to re-open the discussion but quickly ran out of arguments, when it was pointed out to him that they had a time machine, so what was a year? The three scientists agreed that Detective Zadroga could be a neutral party they could trust to keep certain key components and to make sure none of the three might cheat, although it was clear that the measure was for Smith alone.

• • •

It was good being a cop sometimes, Zadroga thought, as he showed his ID to campus security. The keys he had copied jammed a bit—that was to be expected because they were made from clay impressions. Once in the lab, he carefully removed the expensive and irreplaceable optical components from his briefcase; the briefcase that he kept for the group until they could agree on certain ground rules. They would have access to the lab, but without the optical components that Zadroga held in safekeeping, that would prove useless. And Zadroga would not have access to the lab, of course.

After the year was up? Zadroga had already decided that three harmless nerds, easily intimidated by a cute waitress, seemed more reasonable gatekeepers to perhaps the most powerful technology imaginable, than any nation or international power that he had seen.

But who watches the watcher? Through his life in the police force, Zadroga had been incorruptible. So going back in time to buy stocks, or other get-rich-quick schemes, didn't tempt him. But he did have one regret. Not the marriage, for to recast that past event might mean that his daughter—a true light if ever there was one—would exist only in some chaotic limbo.

No, his only regret was that he had once cruelly rejected someone's love.

Ten year before, after being gutted by that psychotic young man in the throes of psychosis, Zadroga had come to know his assailant's sister. At first it was pity; she felt responsible for her schizophrenic brother, and she began visiting Zadroga while he was in the hospital. Later they began meeting for lunch. One day she told him that she felt ashamed, because he was married, but she was attracted to him. He felt the same but never said so and had trusted himself never to act on it. She told him that she first found that she loved his strength, his calm resolve, and then came true love. He felt her love as certainly as one feels a hot fire on a cold night, and yet it was easy, through long practice, to deny himself that comfort.

It all came down to one night. He had gone to meet her at her apartment; it wasn't wise. When he tore himself away, he saw her not as a person, but rather as one more moral test. He stopped her arms before they encircled him, and left feeling the better person. He broke her heart and went home to a house he could now admit was devoid of love.

Looking back, he realized that what he regretted was not his loss, but making the judgment of her and for her. He treated her not as a fellow human being, but as some abstract temptation.

Her apartment building hall was empty; he felt awkward, standing there, waiting. And then he heard the plaintive sobs from around the corner of the corridor. How could he have been so cold? He heard his past-self tell her, he had a wife. Eventually, he heard the carpet-muted footsteps come his way. He stepped back into the corner, shielding his face with his hat and composing his words carefully. Intimately aware of his audience, he would know how to persuade, if not this time, the next. How he'd find his new future upon his return, he didn't know, but if his actions changed only the memory of the past, and he was beginning to think that *that* was all Smith had really done, perhaps it would be worth leaving her a remembrance that he at least tried to place her love above his rules.

Out of Sight

I tried, sitting in the food court of the mall with those knitting needles and a last meal of Bourbon Chicken and an Orange Fanta to wash down the dust of five crushed Dicodids. That was my mistake, the opiates, not the mall. The mall was a stroke of genius, because I'd get faster response than if I'd done it right in the Emergency Room. There they probably would have left me screaming, sitting for hours on one of those hard plastic chairs, with my eyes weeping goo. But not at the food court. No screaming patient would be left for long in *those* hard plastic seats, not with all the shoppers.

But the drugs knocked me out before I could do the deed. Woke up in jail on a drug charge. Then they found my note, and it was off to the loony bin. That's where I thought of the blindfold. I stayed there until they decided I was a faker and a moocher. That was nineteen seventy-nine and I still get hassled by Social Services about the blindfold. *Don't you realize that there are real blind people out there?* No fake modesty here but just to point it out to them, it's just as likely their ass I'm saving. All I ask in return is my check. It seems like a fair bargain. My last councilor thought it would be therapeutic to write my story. My thought was, what the heck, it would also save the constant retelling.

• • •

I hadn't seen Dan in a while. I knew about the accident but it took a chance meeting with his sister to get me to call.

I was on my last week of Unemployment Insurance, and I was the last person I'd have picked to cheer anyone up.

I found his phthalo green, split-shingled insurance-money bungalow along the street of humble single residences. It was a gray mist of an afternoon, in the fifties; a typical October day in the great Pacific Northwest. Wet laurels encroached the cracked and heaving walk that lead up to a tilted porch.

Even through the wavy glass-paned inner and outer door of an enclosed entry, I could see that the distorted shape inside was Dan. He was stooped over, busily arranging something in boxes. In grade school, he was the biggest guy in the neighborhood and we nicknamed him *Baby Huey*. He had that same large cartoon duck body shape.

I rapped; the sharp rattle of loose glass panes made me wince.

Dan turned and came to the door. He opened the first then the second door. We had an awkward moment in that tiny entry, resolved by manly pats on the shoulder.

"Just wanted to see how you were doing," I said. That sort of generic greeting would let me leave quickly if things got weird.

"Hey, cool, come on in," he said, followed by his little *huh, huh* laugh, wrinkling his big face in a self-conscious smile.

Apparently what Dan had been fooling with, when I rang the bell, were bottles of home-brewed beer. This had just become legal in February of that year, thanks to a law signed by Jimmy Carter, and Dan had lost no time. He led me directly into the kitchen and began a tour of the brewery. The aroma was not entirely pleasant. There was another odd smell under that—a lower harmonic of an odor, just out of sensory range—I couldn't quite place it.

Dan claimed, pointing to bulk cans of malt and hops on the shelf, that each beer cost less than eight cents. He may as well have told me he could turn seawater into gold. I couldn't help but think that it was too good to be true, and the big tub and the chrome hand pumps and the clear plastic tubing with a residue of brown sticky liquid, took on a sinister cast, reminding me of a funeral home tour I was forced to go on when I got caught speeding in high school.

We retired to the living room where dozens of cardboard boxes held an orphanage of beer and pop bottles now containing freshly minted quantities of yeasty homemade beer. From an ill-fated youthful experience making root beer, I couldn't help but feel we were surrounded by cartons of unexploded ordinance.

Dan's Fender Jazzmaster electric bass guitar leaned against the sofa.

"You still play?" I asked, pointing to the bass, with its deep red, double-horned body and flesh-colored neck.

In the summer before high school, we formed a basement band that rose no further. We had no name for ourselves, but that wasn't for lack of trying. All attempts at names devolved into bickering. The only thing we agreed on was that all truly great bands had names that began with "The . . ." Dan was the bass player and sang backup. His initial qualification was a 25-Watt Heathkit AA-181 Mono Combination Amplifier that he had put together himself. I remembered the overworked smell it made when I shared it for my guitar. Suddenly I identified the odd smell just under the pungent green-beer odor: Ozone.

He must still be playing with electronics, I thought. Dim as he seemed, and I suppose big lunks always fought that prejudice, he loved breadboarding projects from electronics hobby magazines.

Don picked up his bass and, unplugged, played lines from a Black Sabbath tune. It was bad, like an untalented beginner, but he glowed of self-assurance.

"Wow, Dan, great," I said, feeling like a parent at the finish line of the Special Olympics. The words *brain damage*, formed, unbidden, in my mind.

Suddenly I needed food—any food. My stomach growled, and I actually hoped he heard it. As though psychic, Dan set down the bass and went to the kitchen. He returned with some cold beers, a large bag of salted-in-the-shell peanuts, and a paper grocery bag. He folded the top of the sack on itself to make a waste basket and stretched the filmy peanut bag against his thick thumbnail, until he'd ripped out a gaping hole. Peanuts clattered onto the dark wood coffee table.

It always seems that men, much like their Sumatran male orangutan counterparts, are isolated in jungles of stoicism. However, at times, and those times usually occur in the evening and after copious amounts of beer, there is a need to share, and I could tell that Dan had something to get off his furry chest.

"Want some?" he said. I was already cracking open the next of an ever-accelerating peanut parade.

Knowing the price I'd be paying for the beer and peanuts, it was no surprise when the accident was the first topic. We all listen to such stories with genuine sympathy, but what we really want to know is just how the poor bastard screwed up.

Dan had been alone in a rural area, riding his ten-speed bike, he came around a turn, and a car hit him. The driver drove off, leaving Dan broken and bleeding like a road-kill possum. However, that was just the beginning of his trouble.

I've been known to black out from a well-told compound-fracture story, so I cringed when he launched into the medical stuff. They set his legs—something about pins, broken ribs, and extensive brain surgery. The skull fracture at the back, was a clean crack—Dan actually said that, *a clean crack*. I felt light headed. There must be degrees of *clean* because a splinter of skull the size of a sewing needle had broken off and was driven into the brain tissue.

Bone drills... tweezers... I knew I'd never be able to look at a coconut the same way again. I gazed about the room, at lamps, the beer bottle in my hand, the top album leaning in a box with its cover-art of a vision of hell in orange hues. I wondered if it would be impolite to ask if Dan had some pot.

I grabbed the tail end of a sentence, "Then my sister found me on the floor."

"In your hospital room," I finished with much concern in my voice.

"Huh? No, my parent's house."

I tried to cover. "Right. At your parent's house."

"I was in the second time for a couple weeks but I don't remember much. Then physical therapy and stuff."

"So they missed something the first time?" I was back on track.

"Duh!" Dan said. "They'd sent me home the day after my surgery."

When the lawsuit happened Dan had picked the glossy law firm on the back of the phone book. It was easy to prove diminished capacity. They just put Dan on the stand. Dan just sounded stupid. The cracker was that, besides the loss of fine motor control, he wasn't that bad off. With the settlement, although he wasn't wealthy, Dan would never have to work again.

God, I was jealous.

Thankfully, after a brief *showing of the scars*, we concluded the medical freak-show portion of the evening's entertainment.

Dan played some cuts off albums, showing me what he was into. I hated that stuff: Motörhead, Angel Witch, and the aforementioned Black Sabbath. It was driving and visceral, plus the album covers were horrific and evil.

"Dan," I said during a song about a crank binge in which the singer actually rhymed *amnesia* with *anesthesia*, "This is not a good vibe."

He put on The Beatles' *White Album*, and the sight of the familiar green Apple label rotating slowly on the chrome spindle at thirty-three and a third calmed me.

We were in the middle of "Blackbird" when Dan made his confession.

"I think something's wrong with my brain."

"Isn't that what you got the cash for?" I said more out of surprise than insensitivity. I looked at my watch.

"Okay, sure. It's nothing. Never mind," he said, laughing a little longer than normal. He hung his head like a hurt puppy. I should have known not to look at my watch.

I sighed.

"Sorry," I said, "I have something later," covering my lie with the truth. "It isn't important. So like, what's going on? Like, you can't remember things, you wet your bed, or what?"

"Do you ever see things?" he asked, ignoring my bid at the childish insult that I'd hope would take us back to that time when nothing really mattered.

I sighed again. I didn't come to have a serious conversation.

"Are you, you know, saying that you're seeing things, Dan?"

"Maybe," he pondered. "Don't you ever see things in the air?"

"UFOs?" Only the least bit of a laugh escaped.

"Not in the sky. I mean like in this room."

"Like a ghost?"

"No, it's a bigger deal than that."

"What? Trolls?" I was starting to revert again to our childhood, where the main point of any conversation was ridicule.

"No, it's like it's everywhere." Dan pointed at the blank expanse of wall above the sofa, to the right of a Judas Priest poster. "Don't you see it?"

"Like what Dan, a spider?" There was no spider, but I needed to check. When drunks get the DT's, they see that sort of thing, usually crawling on them. But, the hallucinations from the DT's are what happen when you *stop* drinking and Dan the Brewmeister clearly wasn't in danger of drying out.

"God!" Dan said, standing up.

I had a chilling thought. I'm sitting in a very small living room with a very large guy who could take me apart like one of the peanuts we're shelling.

After a minute, Dan laughed his little chuffing, self-conscious laugh and said, "Not on the wall. It's the air between here and there. Doesn't it seem like it isn't clear, like it's got shapes or things moving in it if you look for a while? It's kind of creepy."

I like creepy. In the basement where we played music as kids, sometimes we'd turn off the lights and have stare-downs in the dark. After a while, the other kid's face would start to distort and become demonic. Your eyes play tricks on you.

I made myself relax. I was on my third free beer, and the music was nice. I leaned back against the sofa and stared at a blank area of the wall by the front door. Your eyes want to focus on the wall, but, after a minute, they get tired. I started to notice that the air was not exactly the calm and crystalline medium through which light rays traversed unmolested.

The first thing I noticed was that there seemed to be a general activity, like snow on a TV channel without a signal. In that faint shadowy seething, some variation developed. Ill-defined shapes appeared unbidden against the backdrop of the wall.

No, I thought, this is just some retinal activity. Nevertheless, I noticed that now, I couldn't *not* see the strange energetic activity in the air.

"Damn it, Dan," I said.

"So, did you see them?" He said.

"Like some shapes... so?"

"No, wait... There!" he pointed excitedly to a spot to the left of the front door.

I saw something. Ordinarily I wouldn't have noticed or simply taken it for an afterimage, but there was an egg-shaped blob like a super-imposed image. It drifted towards the left.

"Dan, which way is it moving?"

He laughed, "To the left."

That felt very weird, but he could have guessed or just watched my eyes. I asked, "So what's it look like?"

"She's beautiful, don't you see her?"

"Shit man, I almost fell for it."

As kids, we were all intolerably cruel to one another, and now I wondered if Dan thought it was his turn.

He rubbed his face and said, "Oh right, I forgot. They looked different when I first started seeing them."

Uh huh.

"Was it like an egg?" He spanned his hand about a foot and a half apart. "About this high?"

Exactly the size I saw.

"Okay, fine." I said, pretending to ignore the ice running up my spine. I picked up a peanut but dropped it back on the table.

Dan stood up and clenched his fists. "I'm not crazy," he said.

Politicians say, *I'm not lying*, prisoners say, *I'm not guilty*, but even back then, I knew that only crazy people say, *I'm not crazy*. I also knew that Dan couldn't keep a joke going for more than two seconds before folding. Like the jury that gave him the settlement based on his apparent impairment, I voted in favor of his veracity due to his shortcomings.

"Why can I see it, if you are the one with the brain thing?" I asked, punctuating with my index finger, feeling like I was having a Perry Mason moment.

"I see it better," he said. "When I got out after the coma, it was like there was always something there, like some reflection on a window. Then I could see things better and better and then... But, maybe it's like Indian scouts in the movies. They find the trail, and then you see it, but only after they point it out."

Unfortunately, it made sense to me.

"Weird," I said. "So is this like some parallel universe that's all around us?" I waved my hand, feeling the air around me, expecting my hand to collide with something the consistency of Jell-O.

"No, it's different all the time, you know like it's always shifting. Sometimes it's scary. I see it *better* when my amp is on and I'm holding my bass. Weird, huh?"

"Yeah, weird, but it must be like an antenna, you know, the guitar."

"I thought about that," Dan said. "I wondered if I could make a better antenna."

"What about turning up the power?"

Dan laughed. He got up and opened the bedroom door. I followed. There were two massive bass speaker cabinets and, on top, an amplifier head.

Dan slapped the amp head and said, "Ampeg, SVT 810E."

I leaned around the back and looked at the spec plate. "Wow," I said. "Is that a joke, sixteen *hundred* watts?"

Dan laughed. "That's stock. I made some improvements."

"Wow," I said. "Turn it on."

Dan looked at his watch. "I can't disturb the neighbors."

"No, I mean just let me hold the guitar. I'll muffle the strings."

Dan got his bass, plugged it in, turned on the amp, and handed it to me. I concentrated. I squinted. "Sorry, Dan, nothing. Show me something, oh faithful Indian guide." I'd been to a Spiritualist Church (actually someone's garage with two rows of folding chairs), the week before with a hoped-for girlfriend, and they all seemed to have faithful Indian guides, with names like Little Flower, or Running Deer. So, I thought that declaration might stimulate things.

Dan peered into the world only he could see and his face darkened. "This isn't one of the good places. But there... look over there."

I looked where he pointed, holding firm to the metal strings. What at first seemed unresolved, fleeting patterns of static, resolved into an image. I saw a large version of something you'd see in a drop of rancid pond water; a rhoto-something, I think it's called. It was still half-imagined, and I was having doubts again. I put on a wolfish grin and asked, "Okay, so what's *that* look like?"

"Like a stem with fingers sticking up, kind of like a crown, and they're all moving around. It's orange with brown near the bottom."

That was exactly what I saw.

"Dan, it's not clear. Maybe it's because you're... you know." I pointed to the back of my head. "Turn it up."

"No!" he said. "One little bump or squeak, and it'll shake the house. I'm not kidding. My neighbors will call the cops!"

"Look, I'm deadening the strings. Turn it up, you baby."

Dan turned the dial slowly up. I felt a powerful, throaty hum in my chest but there was no change in my perception. Dan on the other hand looked like he was in total shock. He quickly turned the volume all the way down.

"Whoa," he said. "That even worked a little without the guitar. Now I'll hold it and you turn up the amp."

"Dan, what if something bad happens, like your brain gets fried?"

"Now you're the baby. I was seeing like this hell-world or like something on that *Angel Witch* cover. I want to see it for real."

His excitement over some hellish vision disturbed me but then I thought, *it's what I like about monster movies.* We were just looking after all. I handed him the guitar and stationed myself by the volume control.

"Ready?" I asked. I felt a little stupid, like when we were kids playing astronauts, except I'd be going from one to ten this time. It was just a little black knob on a bass guitar amplifier. Idiots everywhere played these things with that volume and it didn't seem to... well, actually it did seem to produce some odd lyrics and album covers. I cranked it all the way, to ten. I looked at Dan, and he was rapt. I squinting into the void, wondering what he was seeing.

Strangely, my own vision into this new world also seemed clearer. That plant thing... I could make out the color. It wasn't a healthy color, like a carrot or an orange, but filthy like a schoolyard basketball. All the same, it was the color Dan identified.

Something else I missed because it took up so much of my field of vision: A huge beast on two fat legs, almost manlike, but where the head should be there was just a lump, like a dumpling out of a stew. It was unclear, like a reflection in a store window but I could make out that there were five or six large dark hairs or feelers sticking out of folds of fat on that disgusting head. They were thick at the base and came to points which ended in a short withered thread, like mung bean sprouts that had gone bad.

As I concentrated, it came into focus. Its two arms ended in large hands, each about two feet across, with a thumb and one large opposing index finger terminated by a flattish claw that looked like pine bark. There were two more fingers on each hand. Those fingers were narrower but much longer, having an unnatural number of joints, and they continually furled and unfurled like a roll-up party noisemaker. Liquid seeped from dark tumor-like nodules on its body, and I was thankful I couldn't smell it. Its posture seemed angry or perhaps even haughty, like it was a king. What frightened me was that it seemed to be looking at, and hulking over Dan.

I wanted to run, but Dan seemed frozen.

"Dan," I whispered. "Don't move. I'm turning down the power."

Dan didn't answer.

"Dan," I repeated. "Don't move!"

As I slowly reached toward the volume control, the feelers on the thing's head jiggled violently, and then aimed directly at my raised hand. *Oh God!* I realized it was seeing me.

I reached very slowly for the knob and it reached out at the same speed for Dan's head. The closer I got to the knob, the closer its hand, the great thumb and forefinger opening like a claw, got to Dan's head. I slowly pulled my hand back, and it pulled its hand back. I moved again towards the dial, and it moved to Dan's head. I moved my hand back again, and it opened its fingers wider but did not pull back as far this time. Its body shook a few times, and its fat dumpling head tilted back slightly. I had the distinct impression that it was laughing.

Dan's back was to me and I started to see, at the back of his head, light coming through an uneven fissure. The light turned to ropey tendrils of white vapor, which wound their way towards the creature in front of him. I heard a loud pop from the amplifier and Ozone assailed my nostrils. What had been a deep throaty hum became an ominous buzzing.

"Dan!" I yelled.

"Can't move," he seemed to struggle to get it out.

Illuminated smoke now poured from the crack in Dan's head and drifted towards the monster as though drawn by a powerful vacuum.

"Dan, let go of the bass!"

I made a slow move towards the volume and the monster quickly closed its fingers near Dan's head. I backed off. Then it turned towards me and laughed again. I wasn't liking this game. It was checkmate, and no one would blame me if I ran.

"Can't move," Dan said again, straining to speak. His knees shook uncontrollably. Maybe a seizure in his damaged brain, or maybe it was something this creature was doing, perhaps paralyzing Dan with those feelers.

I backed away. *Maybe*, I thought, *if I backed away from the volume, it would back away from Dan.* But, I also had a plan.

The wall plug was on the far side of the large base cabinets. I could see it from where I was, but I doubted that it could. If I could just get to the plug, I could pull it from the wall and end this nightmare.

I looked away to get my bearings and noticed that when I looked back, the creature had pulled its hand back away from Dan's head a bit, as though confused. The antennae, if that's what they were, writhing like a nest of snakes, and its head was moving from side to side, as though searching. As I stared at it again, it locked onto me. I knew then that somehow it couldn't see me unless I was seeing it. I can't explain it. Maybe it's a quantum physics thing where things won't exist unless they are observed.

"Dan!" I yelled. "Look away! Don't look at it!"

"Turn... it... off!" He struggled.

"I'm trying Dan, I've got a plan."

I closed my eyes, stepped back, and felt for the plug. I feared even looking at the plug would tip my plan. I felt the cord and yanked hard pulling the plug from the wall. The amp gave a thudding *wump*—the last gasp of draining capacitors—and I heard Dan fall to the floor.

• • •

They told me that Dan was electrocuted because of the customization he made to his amplifier, but I can't believe it. Dan had worked with electronics most of his life. They blame me for not pulling the plug sooner and they think I simply watched while Dan was frying. No, I witnessed something a bit more sinister than faulty wiring that day.

Poor Dan. He got every working guy's dream—never to have to work another day of his life, only to have that life end too soon. I would have taken a little brain damage for a life without stress over where my next meal was coming from.

Long after Dan's funeral, I noticed that I could still see vague and undefined shapes in the air; the visual effluvium of some alternate reality that I hadn't been able to see before. And knowing that I would continue to improve, I knew someday I would be observed in return and the bridge between this world and the other made concrete.

Blindness seemed the lesser of two evils. And, although I've achieved that without self-mutilation, I regret that the last thing I saw clearly was a shopping mall food court.

However, the mind is a treacherous landscape. There may be facts I've hidden, even from myself: The creature too was blind. I'm sure of it, now that distance from the events allows memories unclouded by overwhelming fear. I never saw its eyes and I really doubt it had them; perceiving in its own atmospheric milieu by means of wavering feelers (as did also the orange plant-like things) much like a catfish uses whiskers to search the muddy bottom of a slough for morsels to sustain it. Even sharks, with their notoriously poor eyesight, use their electro-sensitive snout nerves to perceive the twitching muscles of their prey.

Given that observation is the first tenuous bridge to the unseen, did I merely forestall my fate in eliminating eyesight, which is only one means of observation? I'm now acutely aware of the imperialism of the sighted. I fear that my nerves, having once been exposed to that other world might grow more and more attuned to its wavelength. Especially if some dark beacon—an intelligence having once tasted human life and salivating for yet another—was building that same bridge from the other side as well.

The blindfold's still working. Problem is, I've had these dreams lately. Lying vulnerable and prone in the dark—all physical doors bolted yet all psychical doors unlocked. In that nightly trance that others call sleep, I sense this world's nakedness to that other world's purview.

I'm in a barren volcanic landscape; the sky is orange. Billows of sooty clouds threaten a rain that never comes. I step carefully on red earth through a field of grey heat-cracked rocks the size of human skulls. Plants with dirty orange feelers explore the breezeless, acrid air. Behind me strikes a bright flash of lightning, casting vivid black shadows on the ground before me. I see my outline and beside me, the silhouette of the beast, a rough claw opens above my head. The dry ground awaits my blood, and even in its shadow I see my silent stalker quivering with cruel laughter. I awake in pitch black and grope the cold hard surface of the nightstand for the blindfold, but it's already on.

If I Should Die Before It Wakes

"That is the reason why half of those who have sailed northward to discover the pole never returned, because it would be a miracle if the Remora, whose number is so great in that sea, did not stop their vessels."

Cyrano de Bergerac, Voyages to the Moon and the Sun, 1677

My name is John Cheswell. I've told my story in bits and pieces in interviews—too many of which in venues that seem to have diminished my credibility and drawn fire from groups of what I can only guess are professional skeptics (in that they seem to have no other occupation on this earth than to pester me). Maybe, as many of my critics have suggested, this is simply paranoia, delusion, or some other psychological problem; for example, I could be anthropomorphizing my subject, *Animalia Cridaria Cubosa*, the deadly box jellyfish. To that critique, I'll add more insults (as did *Hercule Savinien* Cyrano de Bergerac with his comic observations of his own proboscis to aid his unimaginative critics: *'Tis a rock, a peak, a cape, a peninsula!"*) For example: I and my subject (Cubosa) often share the same *plebeius primae impressionis* in that we are both often accused of being drifters when we're actually free-swimmers. And so (a theory might go), in correcting the public misconception of this remarkable sea creature, I find my own redemption. I can see that and I offer it as proof of my faulty motivations. But at risk of further ridicule, I'm still compelled to write what I've witnessed, and hope to God someone does more than just net an easy catch—me and my abundant faults—and actually takes the time to seriously review my observations. I won't be an alarmist and claim that the fate of the world is at stake—only mankind's preeminent role.

To take further wind from my critic's sails, let me clarify that I'm a research scientist but not a doctor. I got pasted by a call-in critic recently, during a radio interview with, *"You're no doctor!"* I've never claimed to hold a doctorate. I do not have a PhD. But that's common among working scientists, even nuclear physicists. I wish to neither overstate nor understate my qualifications. I'm an American marine biologist, now working in Australia, but not a doctor.

I also need to clarify that my research trip was neither paid for, nor approved by AIMS (Australian Institute of Marine Science) where I'm employed. I work out of the HQ in Townsville, Queensland. I'm somewhat tired of the accusation that my discovery—some would say cock and bull story—was paid for by the Commonwealth of Australia. I undertook this research on vacation time. Besides which, I'm still a citizen of the United States and not even eligible for Commonwealth scientific grants.

My purpose is not to gain notoriety, or make money selling books, and certainly not to discredit AIMS, but to alert the public and world governments to a dangerous threat. I understand that my testimony and that of the captain of the vessel New Vista and the two others who witnessed the events that occurred after midnight, the night of September 17, 2008, are hard to believe. Those who were asleep down below, during the incident, wrote it off as freak weather or some other misinterpretation.

Now, as to why I don't publish my findings in an accredited, peer-reviewed journal, that will become clear in reading my account, if you have not already heard it in unfortunate summary on some of my radio or TV interviews. My story does not qualify for submission to any scientific journal because there is no *nullifiable hypothesis* for a personal experience. And, although anyone can repeat my journey, they are likely to fail, given that timing and blind luck played a large factor. The ocean is vast and deep; she keeps her secrets well. Even something (perhaps I should say some *thing*), as large as the city of Melbourne could stay hidden under the waves for a very, very long time. Trust me on that.

Concerning Cubosa

Everyone with more than two brain cells to spark together to create the faint glow of thought thinks they know what a jellyfish is. It is not a *fish*, of course—I need hardly be pedantic about that, and I correct neither children nor adults on it. We like to call them sea jellies or just jellies, but even I slip upon occasion. I still think of Pluto as a planet, and I think *jellyfish* is charming… call me a romantic. Still, you can't lump all gelatinous lumps into, well… one lump.

I was hired by AIMS to study the box jellies specifically. That study is funded for very practical reasons. Although there are many stinging jellies and as many as ten thousand stings from the bluebottle alone, the local *Box Jellyfish*, when it stings, kills. Those it does not kill, often wish they were, the pain is that intense and lasts for days. Although there's only about a death a year, this makes people nervous, particularly tourists. Australia has great beaches and scuba diving sites so it is clearly in the public interest to know more about the Cubosa member of the family. The box jelly is a nuisance eight months out of the year, from November to April, concentrated in northern Queensland.

How it kills people is well known; barbs or nematocysts in long trailing tendrils deliver a cardiac poison that goes straight for the heart muscle. The barbs stick in your flesh and even detached from the tentacles, continue to pump poison, much like a honey bee stinger. The normal diet of the box jelly consists of very small fish, so why nature gives one jelly enough poison to kill several adult humans has always remained a mystery, considering that nature generally errs on the side of *excess* with reproduction, and *conservancy* with predation.

What is not known about this animal is everything else. Literally. We don't know where they go in the off months; we don't know why they don't spread to other areas besides the Northeast tip of Australia; we don't know how they mate. We have learned almost everything we know by observing them in sterile tanks in research institutes and through dissection. The reason for this is simple: They are largely transparent in the water and they don't show up on fish finders. You can't tag a few, like with blue fin tuna, say, and hope you get a call back from the captain of some fishing trawler.

As for me, I'm originally from New Hampshire, always loved the sea, been sailing since I could grasp a tiller. I feel I was enormously lucky in my selection of parents, academics from an old New England family, but they acquainted me with work early on. I held summer jobs on fishing boats and I think what first sparked my interest in marine science was quite literal: I got shocked by an electric eel while dumping a net of the day's catch. That knocked me on my ass and made me respectful of that vast, dark, ancient ocean under the little bobbing corks we called ships and boats. I had to know what other strange creatures existed in that unseen expanse.

Thereafter I took to two tracks in high school. One was wrestling; I was All-State, and that year our entire team swept the finals. The second was, what I'd later know as marine biology, but at the time it was just a fascination with all marine life. For me, every week wasn't just Shark Week, it was Anemone Week, Eel Week—you name it, and I did. I don't have the best memory for people's names but the fire for the sea, that, like a road flare tossed in the water, could not be put out. The names Selachimorpha, Cnidocyte, or Anguilloidei, stuck like barnacles to my memory.

I took both my undergrad and grad in marine biology at Brown. If I ever feel more positive about the future, I'd apply to the PhD program at either Dartmouth or UC Santa Barbara. Seemingly diverse choices, but to me the program really depends not on the reputation of the school, but on whether there is someone there you can learn from and with whom you share research interests. I didn't immediately start my doctorate program because of the paper that got published in Nature (on the visual system of Cubosa. I won't bore you with the details but it is the only jelly with active eyes—twenty four of them—so, considering the prenumerations, I saw opportunity to break new ground in the study of how the nervous system coordinated visual information.) I'm really stating that this was low hanging fruit and that I was merely continuing the work of Dr. Martin at Appalachian, and others. I was, of course, working with the far less deadly *Carybdea marsupialis* box jelly found on the North Carolina coast, but the visual system and basic physiology is the same. The opportunity to do some independent research was enough to tempt me away from six more years of academia.

To finish, I'm not married, I'm short, stocky and have been told I have all the attractive features of a bull dog, without its cuteness. Oh, and I'm balding. You could say the same for Churchill and he seemed to do alright. Despite my homely appearance, women surprise me by seeming to like me (I suspect because I'm attentive to how attractive they are, having already written myself off, and many women like to know that they are the only thing of beauty in the room even when it's just me and my date), but I've been busy with school and my unexpected success.

I've been at the Townsville AIMS office for somewhat over three years, and my job has been more pragmatic than most basic science jobs. Again, if you haven't caught my drift: We don't know shit about these creatures.

Therefore, it shouldn't have surprised anyone that I'd find out something startling. What surprised me was the reaction from fellow scientists, considering that: a) we don't know anything, and b) others make a confident claim that my observations are absurd. Huh? How people claiming to be scientists could be so damn certain about what they don't know baffles me.

I think what the lay person doesn't know is that many jellies swim. True, some simply drift in currents and some will raise sails, poking above the surface, to catch the wind, but many types, such as Cubosa, actively swim after prey.

Granted, this predation isn't as heart-thumping as watching a Great White take a seal in one bite. Rather, the method of locomotion always reminds me of the pumping of a heart, the steady intake and out-jetting of sea water (I am perhaps alone in noting the irony that their toxin is a cardiac toxin). Watching them, it seems like an automated and purposeless thumping, like a heart in a jar that you'd imagine sitting on some mad scientist shelf... *tha, tump, tha, thump*... A microphone in the water records more of a liquid *swish, ka-swish*. It still makes me unconsciously grab my own chest, thinking of the fluid gushing through my own heart. I run the sound to the speakers, to show guests to AIMS, yet, truth be told, I find it unsettling and grow more squeamish every time I hear it.

You think the beating—the intake and expulsion of the sea water—is simply a metronomic reflex until you see them steer towards their prey and see that it is purposeful. They are somehow using their rudimentary eyes (eyes far more complex than a creature with no brain can possibly use, but more on that later) and they actually steer towards objects of interest. It sees its prey and quite actively goes after it. That much is not controversial.

I do my share of public relations at the AIMS labs, and again, the thing that surprises most visitors about the box jelly is that unless you are an Olympic class swimmer, it can out-swim you. If it wanted to chase you, it would catch you and the next thing you'd experience, if you survived, would be the *WOMP!* of electrified paddles at the ER, calling you back from whatever nirvana awaits you at the end of that tunnel. Most injuries and deaths are accidental. It can't control its trailing, nearly invisible, tendrils.

I'm always asked if I've been stung. To paraphrase the old motorcycle wisdom, *there are two kinds of motorcyclists, those who've crashed and those who will.* You get the picture.

I keep several gallon jugs of vinegar sitting around the lab. The barbs can't be seen with the naked eye and brushing against their tendrils is like touching soggy toilet paper, it breaks off and sticks to you. The vinegar stops the nematocysts from pumping venom by dissolving the pumping mechanism.

If someone gets a good dose of venom, they need anti-venom within thirty minutes, although it can be over in three. I haven't been stung that badly, but all that would take would be an extended brush along just one tentacle. People have gotten that from stepping on a recently dead Cubosa, the waves lifting the tissuey tendrils again and again, sticking more and more of them against someone's leg. It's just as if someone unrolled dozens of long strands of toilet paper in the water. Then, as a reaction to the unbearable pain, they reach down to brush it off and engage their hands and arms. That story too often ends in tragedy.

I feel fortunate in that I've had just a few careless brushes against a small part of my arm. It's enough. I've been to the ER a couple times. What does it feel like? Once I was changing an electric plug in my parent's house, I thought I turned off the right breaker and grabbed the fixture to pull it from the wall—I was wrong about the breaker—feels just like that; like grabbing a live wire. Then there is the pain as the poison moves through your lymph system. Heat or ice helps. It doesn't seem to matter which.

As the literature states: *In Australia the Box Jellyfish causes more deaths than snakes, saltwater crocodiles, and sharks combined.*

I don't want to keep people from enjoying the beach and an ocean swim. There have only been eighty-three deaths going clear back to the late 1800's; not even one a year.

My work at AIMS

The nice thing about working in Australia is starting with six weeks of vacation (six rather than the normal four because AIMS was funded by the Commonwealth). And I had six weeks stored up before starting my expedition. I'd worked at AIMS for three years and it was curiosity, rather than the need for a break, that sponsored my vacation. Frankly, I found my work to be its own reward. I also liked life in Northern Queensland. I had few complaints about my New Hampshire upbringing, but I loved Australia. No matter what people may believe about the US, there is a strict class system; not so down under. The people are direct, and they retain the easy sociability of the pub.

As a researcher, you can often learn more things about the local wildlife (in every respect) in a few hours in the local drinking establishment, than you'd never find out, sitting in the lab. I found I got along pretty well, after learning a few simple rules, such as when to duck and when to stand your ground and to always do both with a smile on your face.

I never pretended to be anything I was not. I never attempted the local dialect, yet, after I'd say a year or so, there was an unconscious reduction of long E's to I's that amused my American family on my yearly holiday visits. I tended to frequent Molly Malone's for the Guinness and to watch Australians pretend to be Irish while listening to American rock music.

The whole of Northern Queensland seemed to be about the sea and in particular the Great Barrier Reef. Most occupations, in one way or another, owed themselves to that natural wonder and I found the most wonderful stories from scuba guides and others involved in the tourist industry. Of course, I revealed my origins as soon as I opened my mouth and the Ausies seemed to never tire of prodding curse words from me to match the inflections they'd heard in Hollywood movies. "Say asshole again mate!" "No one says asshole like you Yanks!" I became passable at De Nero, Stallone, and others, if I do say so myself. But it was all in the interest of science, always exchanging a good Godfather quote for another story of a personal encounter with the Box Jelly. Often these stories illuminated previously unlit avenues of my research. I should say how important that alcohol was, for people will only tell you the truly interesting stories when drunk, and perhaps when you're also more likely to accept such stories.

For example, and this is really what started the trouble, a diver for a tourist ship—a two-master, popular for being an all-sail/no-power day tour—told me about an interesting thing he saw. Now, *Steve* I'll call him—not my most favorite person in the world, being one of those local guides who seemed to specialize more in the young daughters of tourists than the local flora and fauna—had learned to be quite observant when diving. It's basic operant conditioning: Steve would normally be equipped with tanks while the tourists would be equipped with a snorkel and floating on the surface, and Steve would go lower, looking for an octopus or some other thing to bring up for the tourists to gawk over, thus insuring Steve a larger tip.

On one such occasion, he told me, he spotted two Cubozoan, which are hard to see, due to being almost transparent in nature, doing what he was certain was a coordinated maneuver. As Steve described it to me, one jelly seemed to be driving a small fish (a juvenile spotted hogfish from what I could take from his description) into the tentacles of the other jelly. Then, after the fish was entangled and stunned, the other Cubozoan did the same for his mate. I would have discounted Steve's story on the spot, except it resonated with something I'd seen in my Cubozoan tank in the research lab. I'd seen it but didn't allow it to register. I don't know if you've had that experience, *observing* but somehow you gloss it over and edit out the inconvenient details it in your conscious mind. It's as though you can't bring yourself to believe what your own eyes see; times when you're both the Galileo and the Pope rolled in one.

Although scientists make their bones discovering new phenomenon, we're also a conservative bunch, and if you do spot something new, there is also an initial *"Oh, Crap!"* moment, where you weigh on one hand the possible, eventual glory of your Nobel Prize and on the other, the years of being burnt daily at the stake for your heretical notions until your new idea becomes canon. I know several research scientists, teaching at Universities, who are sitting on stunning discoveries until they get tenure. Those who thought their grade school playground was cruel haven't met the scientific community.

I spent most of the next year with my jellies in the tanks, looking for signs of cooperative predation. I observed it right away, of course, but that sort of casual observation wasn't going to cut it if I wanted to get published.

The chief research scientist I worked under, Dr. Lowen, an Aussie who had earned his Ph.D. at Scripps, was more interested in coastal ecology, than the research that I was hired to do. I don't mean to imply a lack of responsibility on Lowen's part, but I was largely left to follow my own research; even given signing authority (within the budget of course,) which was generous, due to the perceived importance of my work for the public. It was easy, politically, to justify spending money when the public is being harmed. Much of the equipment I needed was also useful to other researchers at AIMS, and I was never stingy or territorial, so, like some visiting rich uncle, my popularity at AIMS no doubt exceeded my natural charm. I was allowed a latitude and a degree of support from colleagues that most researchers could only dream of.

To prove that the actions of two jellies represented coordinated predation and not random movement, I rigged cameras, working with software (thanks Menkin! Roger Menkin, the institute's general electronics/computer wiz) that would track tags I'd placed on the box jellies against grids I'd taped down on the floor of the tanks.

I had hours of video that Menkin's software reduced to lines I could then chart. I felt I had established that beyond a doubt, but no science journal would agree. I started with the top, *Nature*, and worked my way down the list, collecting enough rejection letters to paper my cubical. It wasn't (the peer review committees explained) that my statistical analysis was wrong; it was rather that I'd failed to explain the mechanism.

How, they challenged, could two brainless gelatinous blobs communicate a hunting strategy? I asked in reply if they were suggesting that the science of statistics had suddenly gone south. The only answer they could give was that they felt I was cherry picking the data; choosing to model selected video segments that seemed to support my contention and tossing out others, or filming selectively.

I'd occasionally ask Lowen to observe, but he would simply peer into the tanks with a half-smile and fully raised eyebrows and state that, "It certainly *seems* they are working together," then launch into some story of a chance meeting an old friend at an airport after just thinking about them, and how we're always in danger of finding meaning in chance events and significance in random patterns.

He was basically saying that my chart's lines and squiggles were Rorschach tests.

I later found out, from Menkin (also the lab's and perhaps the world's expert on the SAS statistical software), that Lowen relied upon others (meaning Menkin) to parlay data into information, and that Lowen himself, although a great scientist, and I take nothing from that, had but a rudimentary understanding of statistics; certainly not the calculus I was doing to show the relevance in action between two or more bodies in motion. But, my respect for Lowen exceeded my respect for Newton (or Leibniz, if you're in that camp), and eventually I put aside my lab studies.

One evening, I picked up one of my carefully plotted multi-colored charts and thought... *hmm, looks like a butterfly, and this one... a dragon.* I wondered if I was possible that I was seeing patterns where none existed. Were the Cubosa corralling their prey, or simply, due to random motion, eventually trapping the poor fish by pure accident?

I had to accept that relationship alone would not prove to the world that Cubosa acted in concert. I had to accept also that it wasn't a reasonable proof, even to myself, without a theory on the mechanism for communication. It took a while to get over that—a while being one night at Molly Malone's, plus a couple pitchers of beer, and a Hemingway-esque wrestling match with a local tough, and something discretion disallows for the telling, involving a waitress I hadn't noticed had an eye on me.

After a day of brown bottle flu, I cleaned house. I rid the office of anything related to my wild conjectures—the entire sorry mess—and dedicated myself to the work I was hired to do.

I went into the field and tried to get better numbers on populations and conditions for both decreased activity and for blooms (blooms are a sudden, localized explosion in the numbers of adult Cubosa). I succeeded in confirming what dozens of researchers had learned before me.

They are most prevalent, November to April (the upside down Aussie Summer.) They hate it when the salinity gets below a certain level, due to rain or wind. A wind pushing against the incoming waves keeps the heavier, more salt-laden water off shore. They swim parallel to the beach, at successive depths, looking for prey. They eat twenty-five percent of their own body weight each day. And they appear to sleep at night, becoming inactive. I used to object to using the term "sleep"—how can a creature, whose brain consists of a simple junction have conscious wakefulness, let alone sleep? One can hardly call its few nerve strands a node and even the most primitive worm has a notochord. (Twelve pairs of eyes and no brain, reminds me of some classes I taught as a grad assistant.) After my adventure, I have changed my opinion and became convinced that what we see as sleep is true dreamless sleep and what we infer as their waking state, may instead be dreaming, and pray they never make the transition from somnambulist to activist.

Sure, I had improved the numbers and therefore slightly improved prediction. The powers-that-be were impressed. They gave me more money. I gained another week's vacation per year. I had thrown my full weight into it like an angry Sumo, and succeeded in jolting jelly-fish science, one centimeter into the future.

I was practically getting knighted for that and yet I felt useless. There were more important issues affecting all jellies, such as global warming, acidification of the oceans, loss of sea turtles, and pollution; all those factors favor Cubosa and other jellies. And jellies compete with humans for food (an accidental introduction of the Comb Jelly into the Black Sea resulted in the loss of an entire fish population.)

Or take any one: Sea turtles are somehow immune from the toxin and are the box jelly's only predators. Or the problem of increased acidity of the oceans; our little subjects survive in 5.5 pH—an acidic condition that kills most other marine life. There is an ocean of study possibilities to choose from. Now that I write this, I wonder if anyone is studying turtles for clues on an antibody or whatever means they use for venom immunity. Yet, casting aside all temptation, I had resolved, for a few years anyway, to be grateful for my own daily bread and stick like a remora to the aims of AIMS. Of course that didn't last.

The Germ of a Dangerous Idea

Every once and a while, a man can have a thought, so ruinous to his life yet so unavoidable; as though you contracted a virus that simultaneously gave you the flu and cured baldness. I picture Galileo espying the non-Aristotelian imperfection of the craters on the moon, and exclaiming... however one said *Oh crap!* in Italian in those days.

My heretical journey began here.

To be the science geek a moment: Most sea animals, such as salt water fish, react poorly to fresh water due to an osmotic balance to uric acid (the exception being the Bull Shark which has an organ dedicated to dumping excess uric acid and has been found thousands of miles up fresh water rivers). Cubosa is no exception but its reaction to even minor reductions in ocean water salinity is way out of line. They will flee an area if the salinity drops even a little. Yet, they aren't physiologically damaged by low salinity. So why do they avoid it?

I found I could get them to move out of an area in the tank, simply by pouring in a liter of fresh water. That effect is non-controversial. I typically kept three or four Cubosa per tank, fed regularly with whatever small fish were convenient. I noticed a sluggish hunting response in those who were in lower salinity tanks. Yet, when there was just one Cubosa per tank (an all too frequent situation, I suppose for the same reason that my house plants never survived), there was no difference in survival rates between the preferred salinity levels and the low salinity levels. What that meant, and it took me months to realize the obvious, was that, in noting the time it took to capture prey, when there were more Cubosa in high salinity, they seemed to have an advantage in capturing live food. However, the low-salt Cubosa showed no numerical advantage (more Cubosa did not lead to more effective predation beyond simple chance). In fact, the high salt Cubosa showed an *exponentially* greater effective predation; four weren't twice as effective at hunting as two, it was more like six times more effective.

That kept gnawing at my attention like the rustling sound of a stubborn luffing you couldn't trim out of a poorly rigged mainsail.

Inspiration comes from the oddest places sometimes. Like I said, I'm a good sport at AIMS and show my lab to visitors—give them the big scare stories. I was with such a group, some councilwoman and her family, and pointing out how much the pumping jelly bodies remind one of a beating heart, when, out of the mouth of the Councilwoman's eight year old son. He said that the floating jellies and their tendrils reminded him of brain cells—neurons! He'd just seen some TV science show about the brain. Well, I just about fainted. Seriously, I had to grab the edge of a nearby desk. I rushed through the rest of the presentation—some of my best material—and shoved them off on Maxwell and his sharks. Then I called Menkin. I needed someone with an engineer's mind.

Perhaps it was something in the tone of my voice on the phone, but within seconds, Menkin burst through the door, almost breathless.

With only my briefest outline, Menkin grasped it at once. Or I had to assume he did, because sat down and got one of those far away looks, and didn't appear to be breathing for some time. Then he asked, "These blooms, how big do they get?"

He was asking about the blooms. That is where, when conditions are right, a jellyfish (not just Cubosa) will erupt from polyp to full adult. Thousands of tiny, unseeable polyps will become a huge colony, sometimes infesting beaches and making them unusable, or as in Japan, giant Numuras (over six feet across and up to four hundred pounds each) can invade the sea of Japan and totally disrupt fishing, or, as happened one year, clog inlets to a nuclear plant. And again, as with the turtles and the Cubosa, this is due the decline of species who normally prey upon the Numuras (although in this case, it is fish who eat these jellies in the polyp stage).

I told him, it depends. A bloom could be a few hundred, or, like the Moon Jellies in the Gulf of Mexico, so many it looks like you could walk on them for a hundred nautical miles.

"But these?" he asked, pointing at the Cubosa in my tanks with his long sharp nose. "A million, say?"

I didn't know. They don't float on the water, so the extent of a bloom can only be guessed at by the numbers that show up at a beach. The problem, I told him, was that you can't just use sonar to locate them. Where they go and what they do, remains a mystery.

"Why's that important?" I asked.

"If it is, as you suspect—that these seemingly individual animals are actually cells in a larger collective, communicating, much as our own neurons but via the conductive medium of seawater... well!"

"Well?"

"Well! I'm sure you are aware that in the AI community, there is no little discussion of node numeracy and self-emergent consciousness."

I wasn't ready for that. I had just been wondering about why two jellyfish seemed smarter than one and communication via seawater seemed to solve that; I was simply thinking of simple nerve impulse. Because it explained why Cubosa were a better hunters when there were more than one... *but*, only when the water salinity stayed above a certain point; a point at which electrical signals traveled easily. Of course pure or distilled water does not conduct electricity at all. But then Menkin had to hit me with that; The question of how many jellyfish, as de facto neurons, it would take to form a *brain*. This was all because a bunch of AI hardware geeks have the idea that if they just give a PC enough RAM, it will become self-aware. It made my head spin. But Menkin had just started his damage. Yet he would be both innocent and ignorant of how his next statement would explode in my head.

It was three in the afternoon. I locked my lab door and turned off the main lights so it looked like I wasn't there. My basement lab was then lit by a couple desk lamps and the lights in the jellyfish and bait tanks. I remember everything about that afternoon. I went to the cooler, opened up the freezer door and grabbed the unopened bottle of Stolichnaya I'd kept in there; a gift from someone at the lab Christmas party. I rinsed my coffee mug, proffered a Styrofoam cup from beside the coffee maker and poured a hit for Menkin and then a larger dose for myself.

"Wowser," I choked out after a hearty swallow. I remembered then, why I don't like vodka and why the Stolichnaya had been in there, untouched, for all those months. Still, it had the desired effect. Menkin poked at the liquid in his puffy white cup with an index finger, examined the end of his finger in the light, and then took a cautious sip. Daily, Menkin seemed intent on proving that men really were from Mars.

"Mmmm," he warbled. "They seem to do a good job of eliminating the fusil oils in the distillation process."

I told him that the Russians knew what they were doing when it came to vodka; I just wanted to get him back to the topic at hand.

"Well, of course they would, wouldn't they." Milken picked at the edge of his cup. "Do you know what I think the AI folks miss?"

"What?"

"Frequency."

"Like how many megahertz?"

"Yes, but no, I mean a collective and unifying frequency, like brain waves. Entrainment."

"Everyone marching to the same drummer."

"Right, nonlinear electrostatic oscillations forming oscillons." He saw my puzzled look. "Self-sustaining frequencies, like brain waves. You know, like Delta frequency, one cycle per second and you're unconscious... dreamless sleep, and..."

"Wait," I had to interrupt him. "You're saying *what* about jellyfish communications? Because I'm going to need your help in designing electronics to pick up—what should I call it—inter-jelly communications?"

"Depends on what you mean by communication."

I tried not to get frustrated with Menkin. It seemed obvious to me: You could almost think of it as inter-cellular communications. I'm no neurologist but the neurons have little branches and they almost, but don't, touch other branches from other cells. But, there is a fluid and neurotransmitters, such as acetyl-choline bridge that gap, and... well, it's complex, but these jellyfish cells—so to speak—are in a conductive medium already: Seawater.

I said, "Seawater conducts electricity. So if they communicate, they create and also receive electrical impulses. It seems to me, that we should be able to pick up the communication, right?"

"I seriously doubt it."

Menkin took things very literally so it took a long back-and-forth to get us to consensus. The problem Menkin saw is that there is an electrical signal in the water upon any muscle movement. Even a near microscopic shrimp produces an electric signal in the brackish, murky water where the platypus makes its home; enough for the sensitive receptors in the platypus's duck-like bill to pick up the signal. Shark's snouts do the same; any muscle flexing produces an electrical signal. So, that meant that simply finding an electrical signal in the water was not meaningful.

Menkin was fixating on the meaning of *communication*, and rightly so. What I had wanted to show was a meaningful sharing of visual information between Cubosa, and I had to agree with him: Isolating, decoding, and proving that it was visual data and not an artifact of muscle movement, would be impossible. We gave up on that.

What we did decide was that coordination could be proved if we simply showed a shared frequency of electrical activity between two or more Cubosa. This would be much as our own brains coordinate by establishing an overall brain frequency. We have Delta, unconsciousness; Theta, dreaming; Alpha, relaxed; Beta, alertness. They go from one cycle per second (unconscious dreamless sleep) to forty per second (you're being chased by a bear.)

I was intrigued with the notion and I wonder if Menkin understood the significance: Consciousness was not only dependent upon the number of nodes but also the coordination, or entrainment under a common frequency. And also that that frequency be rapid enough to allow a continuity of self, much as a series of film images go from being single pictures, to be perceived as a smooth movement after a certain speed.

Our simple plan was to look not for coordinated behavior (as I had done but could not prove) but rather to simply prove the existence of coordinated waves of electrical impulses (brainwaves, in a sense). It seemed like a simple plan, yet I had no idea that this knowledge would prove useful in the future. Knowledge, without which, I wouldn't be here today, and neither would the crew of the New Vista.

The Great Garbage Patch

We were getting some results, working with a few Cubosa in my tanks with the new equipment that Menkin and I had constructed. But it was proving frustrating. We'd see a correlated brainwave function for a while and then it would disappear. Although statistically significant, I knew from my papers on team hunting that I'd get hammered unless the proof was overwhelming.

I also couldn't really take it into the field where there was an opportunity to find a large collection, perhaps even a bloom. Normal observation was of individuals just off popular beaches. They were hard to locate and not really something that you could pick out using a fish finder.

Then I read about someone using DIDSON (Dual-frequency IDentification SONar) successfully to count *Aurelia aurita* jellies in a brackish lake, somewhere in Indonesia. That was ground breaking, or I should say a sea change, I suppose. The old method of netting and counting depended upon first finding a bloom. The DIDSON was finally, in effect a fish-finder for jellies. Problem was, I didn't have one and, despite my rock star status, could not get AIMS to acquire one in a timely manner (they were very expensive, and there was a backlog on order and AIMS was at the end of a budget cycle). So, I was lifted by a high tide, only to be beached.

I tried to think about where the Cubosa may go during the winter months. I knew they were adept swimmers, but no one really knew how far they traveled. The seemingly delicate Monarch butterfly takes its yearly migration from Canada to Mexico; who knows what was possible for Cubosa? It had to be someplace free of both predators and competition. I knew they survived in low oxygen environments that would kill most marine life, and that they preferred near dead calm (waves and wind work to unexpectedly reduce water salinity.)

The perfect spot would be the North Pacific Gyre. This was a place, far north of the Hawaiian Islands, surrounded and yet abandoned by ocean currents and winds; a dead spot in the ocean. It was also famous for the so called "Great Pacific Garbage Patch," popularized as an island of discarded plastic, the size of Texas. There was no doubt it being the size of Texas, but rather than being some new continent (I'm sure that some imagined striding across a new land of plastic bottles and headless Barbies) it was rather a mealy stew of half sunk bits of plastic, in the western Pacific Ocean (between Hawaii and California). You could probably sail through it at night and not really notice. Most it had been ground into tiny particles and broken down by UV rays—it could not be seen by satellite—all of it floating just a few feet under the surface The gyre itself, the slowly swirling area surrounded by ocean currents, is a larger area stretching between California and Japan

The Great Garbage Patch, I had thought, would be the perfect place for Cubosa to winter, ala Brer Rabbit's briar patch.

I had, of course, considered, with my liberal stored vacation time, renting a sail boat out of Hawaii. Two problems: 1) It is a dead sea. The doldrums as they called it in times of yore, so I'd need a power boat, and at today's fuel prices that was out of the question. 2) Although young teens have made news with solo world circumnavigations on sail boats, that doesn't fit my idea of boating safety; that combined with the rigors of doing scientific experiments. Again, I was both raised and beached by the same wave. I had a great idea of where to look for off-season Cubosa but I didn't have the means.

Just reading the news one day I saw that Scripps Institution of Oceanography was sending a ship to examine the Great Garbage Patch. The four-week mission was two-fold: A survey of sea life to determine the impact, and a commercial venture. Brita Water Filter Company (one of the project backers) wanted to see what it would take to recover the plastic. There was tons of it and it represented an almost infinite supply of plastic (an estimated hundred million tons) that started collecting since the day some kid first tossed a plastic toy soldier or *Cracker Jack* novelty into the ocean. It could start a new industry to return the plastic into the petroleum from whence it came. It was all preliminary, and perhaps simply a publicity stunt for Brita. That didn't stop me from looking up every classmate and friend of a friend until I found someone who could get me on board.

Cubosa may have always been drawn to this same dead area; the center of the gyre vortex. But now that warming waters and pollution were diminishing their main predators, sea turtles who have a natural immunity to Cubosa's proteinaceous toxins, it may have made that area a jellyfish Eden. About this same time, my order for the DIDSON had finally gone through, and I was anxious, in more ways than one, to see what the DIDSON equipment would show. I had it drop shipped to the first port of call where I expected to join the expedition.

The Voyage of the New Vista

The main concentration of plastic was in an area roughly 700 nautical miles across, within the gyre that was bordered by ocean currents spinning in a counter clockwise direction (or anti-clockwise as my Aussie associates would say). I met up with the New Vista in Honolulu, the target area being due north of the Hawaiian Islands.

During the day I either slept or helped out where I could. My station was at night. Most self-mobile jellies have a curious habit related to a phenomenon first noticed by WWII sonar operators. They were at first thinking that a thermal layer of the seawater rose and fell with the night and day. It was shown later that this was plankton, shrimp, and other tiny carnivorous marine life, rising at night to feed on the photoactive life that floated near the surface. They rose at night when it was dark and fish could not see them as well. Along with them followed the jellyfish. Such was the extent of this layer of life that it registered on even the most primitive sonar.

As I said, Cubosa and others are self-propelled. I think I read somewhere lately, and it is hard to believe, that there are so many jellyfish, swimming in the ocean, rising at dusk and going down in the day, that they act as a mixer in the ocean, mixing the layers. I tried it myself by putting dyes in the tank and it was quite amazing.

One day, I did a quick calculation of the thrust of one Cubosa, wondering how many it would take to pull a row boat, if you could harness them like horses to a carriage. About a thousand. It wouldn't go fast and probably wouldn't go against even the slightest current. It's about equivalent in numbers, I think I figured, to how many bees it would take to push a car. But, get enough of them and you have a force to be reckoned with, especially considering that a bloom could be in the millions.

So, on the night of September 17, I did what I had done for the previous seven nights, I lowered the DIDSON transducer array off the back of the ship along with the jellyfish *brain-wave* sensors that Menkin had created for me. I had planned to use the pan and tilt pole, but the main layer of particles didn't thin out enough until you got under about thirty feet, so I rigged everything to an underwater equipment sled attached to a winch.

The New Vista was a two-hundred and seventy-nine-foot ship with a thirty-six foot beam. It had a nominal crew of twelve, but, for this trip, we bunked thirty-one with only minor discomfort. My bunkmate was a techie named Jonah

Tuvason (don't think he didn't get his share of teasing about whales.) Having him for a bunkmate was fortunate because he was fascinated with the DIDSON equipment and would often stay up for a while and help me with the setup, or would wake in the middle of the night, just to check on my readings. Jonah was the main operator and tech for the ship's scientific sonar system, a Knudsen 320B/R using two hull-mounted high frequency transducers and a sixteen element array TR-75J transducers for low frequency, and all the computers and recording and printing equipment that went along with that. It was all state of the art but couldn't give the camera-like resolution that the DIDSON could.

On this evening, I had set up the DIDSON myself. Like I said, I'd lowered the transducer array, and off it went into the water from the winch deck which extended from the 01 aft deck. That was also was where, what we called "the trailer" sat. It was a converted shipping container, I guess about twenty feet long, a mobile lab containing electrical and sensor hook ups and communication with the bridge (visual via monitor, if needed). There were other, larger labs on board, but I was using this one because it made the hook-up to the winch easier.

I called up the bridge to check in and got the on-duty officer on the closed circuit monitor. I was surprised to see Captain Andy (so we all called Captain Anders) standing behind him. I wanted to but did not ask the captain what his business was in front of his crew member. He was holding what looked like a steaming hot cup of coffee, so I thought he might be up for the night.

The captain walked up to the camera. "Good fishing, Cheswell? If you're lucky, it's jellyfish flambé ala squid for the crew." He was prone to say something along those lines as a closer every time he found himself in conversation with me and had something to rush off to, which was pretty much every time. It wasn't just me; he knew what a conversation with a scientist was like and kept them to a minimum. So, I returned a chipper, *aye sir*, and punched the off the comm. Then I remembered that since early afternoon we had been heading into other waters, where they hoped to find a denser concentration of sludge (as we had begun to call the soupy plastic debris). That was probably why he was up there, watching like a mother hen.

The captain hated having his ship plowing through the sludge, and that was another thing you heard from him with frequency. You could lean over the rail and see the dirty bits of plastic, ground up from decades of grinding: The plastic case from a 1950's transistor radio against a discarded toy truck; a G.I. Joe doll against a broken smoke detector; discarded medical ventilation tubing against a cigarette display case, all grinding with almost imperceptible slowness in the vast vortex at the center of the gyre.

Those bead-like bits of plastic were not only clinging to the sides of the ship, the awful particles clung to every piece of test equipment that entered the water, and no matter how carefully the crew rinsed things off, in just a few short days, it was all over the ship again, like it was beach sand tracked in by an army of kids on holiday—no, worse, it clung with a static force even after drying. You'd see bits of it on your hand, when taking a bite of food—you'd find it in your food, in your shoes, your hair. It was oily and disgusting, and dingy, having lost whatever bright consumer attracting color it may have once had. I decided that if the jellyfish wanted this part of the sea, they were welcome to it.

Around nine that night I saw my first sonar picture of what I thought might be a Cubosa. We were heading north-northeast at about ten knots and the low drone from the twin D398 diesels was threatening to put me to sleep. I just caught the last of it before it disappeared off the edge of the

DIDSON's bright blue, v-shaped scan area on the monitor. Then I saw another. The outline was unmistakable. I just had a blue monotone image to work with, but it was unmistakably Cubosa.

The resolution was remarkable. I had the DIDSON's transducers on a pan & tilt mount with the transducer maybe twelve feet under. The Cubosa looked to be another ten to fifteen feet under that and I could still make out the bell and the propellant flexing of the velarium, the rhopalium, and even the trailing tentacles, quite clearly. I leaned forward and kissed the computer monitor.

Then I saw two more. Within an hour I was seeing a regular parade of Cubosa showing up at about every twenty feet or so, judging by the range markers that ran along both sides of the wedge that the sonar covered. Oddly, some were going in one direction, about thirty degrees off our current heading, and as many going the opposite direction. I observed this for about thirty minutes before calling the bridge.

The captain listened to my request for a course heading calmly. I had aimed the camera we were using for video communications at the computer monitor that was showing the feed from the DIDSON.

All he said was, "Does it not stand to reason, according to your theories about this creature, Mr. Cheswell, that they would conglomerate at the point of greatest sludge density?"

I wasn't aware that the captain knew or cared about my research or the reason for my being on his ship. I said, "It does."

"We're currently headed to what Dr. Murray H. Grohol, *P, H, D*," he said, emphasizing each letter, "has predicted will be the area of greatest sludge density. Are you asking me to change course based on your non *P, H, D*, reasoning?"

"I am."

"Mr. Cheswell, I'm looking at your jellyfish right now on your monitor. What would you say if I told you that I think your jellyfish know more than Dr. Murray H. Grohol, P, H, D and you combined. What do you say to that?"

I smiled and said, "Thirty degrees to port, then captain."

"Aye, Mr. Cheswell, thirty degrees to port it is," he said. "Will that be all Mr. Cheswell?"

"Aye, aye captain," I saluted, although the camera was still aimed at the DIDSON display.

Over the next hour, I watch the subtle change in the density of the jellyfish. At about 2 am, there was a knock at the door. I got up and opened it. It was Jonah.

"Take a look!" I said, pulling him into the room.

"Wow!" He was impressed. This was for two reasons, one was the obvious, the number of Cubosa. The second was that he'd never really seen what the DIDSON could do. Due to the general lack of sea life, all we had seen up to that point was the occasional recognizable plastic object that had not yet been ground up. It was one thing to see the remarkable three dimensional clarity on say, a discarded computer mouse, it was another to observe the detail it could produce when the subject was a living animate being.

We watched until what must have been about three am. I had been changing the recording DAT tapes. We were using one for recording the DIDSON output and the other for the electronic readings, so I wasn't at the monitor. I heard Jonah exclaim something, *hey*, or maybe he said my name, it was the sharp tone of alarm I remember most. Almost simultaneous to that, I felt the ship lurch a bit. Not much, just enough of a slowdown for me to touch the desk to keep my balance. I'll never forget what I saw next.

Keep in mind that we were trailing the DIDSON display aft, although it was viewing fore. The visual field was just a mass of Cubosa. My first thought was that a group had decided to attack the transducers. But I could see that the camera was still dragging slowly through a thick bloom of them. There was some space between them but not enough to be able to see more than a few feet, to the next jelly. I wondered if that was why we slowed. Could a jellyfish bloom, really slow a ship the size and power of the New Vista? Knowing how fragile and insubstantial the animal was, I refused to believe it.

The captain came on the comm link.

"Cheswell... I see Tuvason there. Either of you swabs lower anything big in the water without telling me?"

"Captain," Tuvason said. "It looks like the jellyfish are so thick it's slowed us down."

"I don't think so," I said. "You'd need so many that..." I started to give my reasons when there was another lurch, not strong, not like when you're standing on a bus that slams on its breaks, but still, stronger than the last one. This was followed by a low moaning from below decks. I looked up at the monitor to see the captain's face go from placid to angry. He was looking at something out of the frame of the camera, perhaps some ship's readout.

"All stop!" he barked. And the ships moaning sound stopped.

I had a sudden fear that perhaps the water intake for engine cooling was being blocked by jellyfish. I asked the captain if that were the case.

"What? No, of course not. Don't bother me right now." He had picked up a clipboard and I saw him writing notes and looking at read outs. He was slowly gaining composure and said, in a calm voice while he carried on, "No, because the Vista uses a closed coolant system with heat exchangers that use another closed system using the ship's ballast." He said that in his reassuring nothing-to-worry-about captain's voice. "You think I'd bring this plastic sludge into my ship? And..." He seemed to check some other readouts. "We are definitely...not... overheating. Hmm..."

"So?" I replied.

"We are obstructed. I think Mr. Tuvason is correct. Your jellyfish, en mass, have us bogged down."

"Captain, that's not possible."

"Cheswell, I don't mean to be rude but you need to stick your Goddamn head out the door of your lab and take a look. And that would be on your way to the bridge. Now! You too, Tuvason. And Cheswell?"

"Yes captain?"

"Take a route to avoid topside as much as you can on your way." He then punched off the comm link.

Jonah and I looked at each other. Jonah said, "Weird," beating me to it by a fraction of a second.

"Wait," I said. I brushed by Jonah and went over to where I'd set a small laptop that I was using to process the electronic data before recording it on to the DAT. I hadn't looked at it. I didn't even have a window open. We were using a basic oscilloscope program that Menkin had tweaked a bit for our purposes. The window opened, looking as you'd expect an oscilloscope screen to look, especially one hooked up for an EEG, its bright green line looking like a dancing mountain range. It was just like a human brainwave pattern. I was stunned for a moment and Jonah had to grab my arm to get me moving.

The trailer opens toward the center of the ship but we had a good view off the back of the flat winch deck. It was a clear night and the starlight and the light from a half-moon, illuminated our surroundings with a cold blue light. All was still. There were no engine sounds nor even the sounds of waves lapping the sides of the boat.

"Do you see that?" Jonah whispered, pointing into the sea.

I peered and realized that what I had though were waves—I could see the peaks catch the faint light—had an unnatural motion to them. It was hard to define, as though seeing an untrained sculptor's attempts to mimic a natural slope and feel of water in motion. They seemed to peak too rounded and stayed up too long to be a natural wave phenomenon.

I saw one wave near us, rise and then stay risen, actually growing taller. When it got high enough, it became translucent enough for me to see that it was made up of hundreds of individual bodies of Cubosa, rising ten, then twenty feet above the sea. To attain that height, there must have been a supporting upwelling, beneath them, of thousands Cubosa, furiously pumping and churning. I thought of all those eyes, twenty-four per jellyfish, and thousands looking out at us now, now level with Jonah and I. We were standing on the aft winch deck, which was itself a good fifteen feet above the sea. More seemed to join in the mound which I could see was now moving directly towards us.

I felt a chill deep in my gut, as though I was about to crap a block of solid ice. Jonah and I backed away, walking backwards to the ladder that would take us up to the door into the safe confines of the 01 interior hallways. I banged hard into the ladder rail and spun around and started climbing. When I looked down, Jonah was pawing the air behind him, trying to acquire the ladder blindly with his right hand, refusing to take his eyes off the ever growing column that now seemed high enough to come crashing down on us, though we were, some twenty feet from the stern.

I could see Cubosa losing their purchase and falling, tumbling from the height and down the sides like boulders down of a quaking volcano. I held on with one hand, then reached down and grabbed Jonah's arm by the wrist and forced his hand on the ladder railing. The mountain of Cubosa, each with enough venom to kill thirty men, tumbled towards us, even as Jonah's feet found the rungs and we began to ascend the ladder. I reached the top and spun around to help him up. Then the wave hit.

The Cubosa and their carrying wave of water crashed, peaking just below me, at about waist high for Jonah. It smashed him to the ladder. He screamed as jellyfish and flaying tentacles flew everywhere. One even flew over the rest and narrowly missed me, skidding off on the deck to my left. I still had a hold of Jonah's arm and could see the wave, jellyfish pumping, but beginning to suck in only air, yet pumping like crazy trying to keep their watery appendage together. I pull him up with all my strength and finally there was a huge sucking sound as the living wave lost its purchase and finally dissolved into individuals, all falling in a heap, on the deck below.

I wrestled the now limp Jonah up the rest of the ladder and lay him down. He had a gash on his forehead; the sheer weight of the column of Cubosa had smashed him against one of the ladder rungs. Bits of jellyfish tendrils clung to his jeans—I didn't know if they'd penetrated or not—and fortunately I saw that he must have zipped up his nylon windbreaker when we left the lab. As I dragged him to the door, he roused and said, "My leg!" trying to grab at his right leg. I held his arms, fast above his head to keep his bare hands from touching the poisonous tentacles while I dragged him through the door.

"What the hell?"

I turned; it was Bream, one of the Brita Water hires. He was holding a pipe.

"I was just going out to…" Bream said, gesturing with his pipe.

"I can see that! Help me with Jonah. And don't touch him from the waist down." He gave me an odd look so I said, "Nemocysts from a box jelly… I don't know if they've fired or not, or penetrated his clothing, but I guarantee, you'll be the sorriest person in the Pacific if you touch one."

I had Bream keep the half-conscious Jonah's hands above his head. The starboard lab was close by. There, I picked up a gallon jug from the store of vinegar I had stored there and called the bridge. I didn't bother to explain what happened, only that Jonah had been dashed against the ladder and was injured. The captain would rouse the medic. Then I ran back, doused Jonah's clothing and carefully removed his jeans and jacket. I saw signs of only minor stinging but both of his knees were beginning to swell and discolor, most likely from the impact with the ladder. Leaving Bream in charge again to wait for the medic, and telling him to not, under any circumstances, open the door to the outside, I ran to the bridge on the 02 level. On the way I felt the ship shudder and pitch forward. It caught me off guard and I fell forward. My right knee hit the hard steel floor of the passageway before I could stop myself. It hurt like hell but I didn't think it was injured and I kind of ran/limped the rest of the way.

The bridge has a commanding view of all open decks on all sides. When I arrived, the spotlight was on the foredeck and I could see it was covered with stranded yet still writhing Cubosa.

"You just missed the show," the Captain said.

"So that's what that was." I shuddered to imagine the wave that the communal mass of jellies must have mounted to be able to land so hard on the foredeck. "I caught the opening number on the winch deck."

The captain seemed calm, but the officer on watch had a look I've seen before. His skin looked palorous and clammy, and his mouth was working like a carp out of water. The captain turned to him and did probably the best thing he could to help the man. He handed him a clipboard and told him to record all readings from the various dials and displays, such as wind speed, barometric pressure. Then he turned to me and stood with his face inches from mine.

"Do you consider this to be normal behavior in jellyfish, Mr. Cheswell?"

"No, sir." Saying *sir* was a compulsive reaction; of course I wasn't under the captain's command. The truth was though, that I felt guilty when he asked that, as though all this was my fault. The truth was that I had withheld information, and in my mind, I did feel responsible. It hit me all at once. I should have known. Here was one of the sea's most abundant, ancient, and dangerous predators. Who would *not* predict that, upon forming a collective thought, that thought might be aggressive? I stood there a moment feeling pretty low.

"You were not honest concerning the purpose of your research." He didn't wait for an answer. "You sir, are responsible."

"I am," I confessed.

"No Mr. Cheswell! I don't think you understand." His captain's hat was sitting on a small chart table, nearby. He picked it up and put it on my head.

"What's your plan, son? You'd better Goddamn have one. Because this is currently not a ship. I can't steer it, make it go forward or aft. This is a useless hunk of metal. Until it's a ship again, it's your show."

It was so dramatic, I had to wonder if he was serious, but one look at his face said differently. He had a look in his eye that said to me, *if you don't get us out of this, the last thing I'm going to do is to kill you with my bare hands.*

I cast my eyes downward, took off the hat and set it carefully down on the ledge above the sonar display. It was now four in the morning. Through the window I caught a glimpse of slowly mounting water on the starboard side. They'd try an attack from another angle. I didn't know if they had the collective strength to overturn a ship of this size, but I didn't want to find out. I thought for a moment.

"Captain, where did you take on your ballast water?"

"Where did I what?" he asked, incredulously. I thought he'd kill me right there.

"Look," I really erupted. "You put me in charge. Answer the question!"

"San Diego... Nimitz Marine Facility."

"A port, a bay, at a quay?"

"San Diego Bay."

I tried to picture it... I had no idea.

"Is it an estuary?"

Surprisingly, the captain of the watch, I don't recall his name, looked up from his clipboard and chimed in.

"It's almost enclosed, seawater, not fresh. We're a little over a nautical mile from the outlet to the sea."

"You just said outlet?"

"Well," he looked over to the captain before continuing. "Several creeks, like Chollas Creek, and some others feed into San Diego Bay. That's fresh water of course. But the main fresh water is from the Sweetwater river."

"Sweetwater! How much ballast?"

He started to do some quick calculations on the clipboard, but the captain spoke up.

"Four-thousand gallons in the forepeak, same in the aftpeak tanks. Then there's two holding nine-thousand each and two more with five, so that's…"

"Thirty-seven thousand gallons," the officer on watch said tapping his clipboard.

"Yes, and then over six thousand in wash water—that's not saline—and two of potable."

"Look," I said. "If we can knock the salinity down, around the ship, only by a little, they will flee the area. How fast can we start pumping ballast and what's the flow?"

"A lot faster than it takes to fill the sea chests. You know how gravity works, don't you Mr. Cheswell? The sea chest inlets and main ballast tanks are at the rear. I'll be taking my hat back now, Mr. Cheswell, if that's all right with you."

"Aye, sir," I said, handing him is hat. I was keeping an eye on the mounting sea to starboard; it was as though they figured the need for a wider base. There was a swell forming, almost the length of the ship.

"I see it," the captain said. "Open all sea chest doors." Then he, as though following his own orders, unlocked a control panel with a key he produced from his right pants pocket. He threw several of the large switches there.

"Why not just the starboard?" I asked. He just pointed to his hat. The officer on watch explained what should have been obvious to me. That would have made us list dangerously to one side if there were jellies pressing on one side and not the other.

The officer of the watch spoke up. "Captain. As soon as this clears the area around the propellers, maybe we should try backing up. But how will we know if this is working?"

"Mr. Cheswell guarantees it. But it would be good to know the moment we can engage propellers." He looked at me.

"I'll go back to the winch deck lab. I should be able to see."

"Very good." The captain turned to stare out the starboard window at the slowly mounting sea, his hands clasped behind his back.

When I got to the lab I immediately saw there was now a void around the DIDSON transducer and from what I could see, around the entire stern of the ship. It had been dragged behind on the sled, but now that we were stopped, it sank and pointed straight up so that I could clearly make out the ship's propellers and we were free to move. I called the bridge with the excellent news. They could now see it as well on their sonar. And the captain told me that the big wave I'd seen when on the bridge, built to a threatening height but then collapsed when it neared the ship and the lower saline water.

We backed up until once again engaging too many Cubosa, then we'd stop and let enough time pass to dilute the water. It was slow going but we were gaining. The Cubosa seemed to realize that. They tried a few attacks but after several further attempts, they seemed to give up and we hadn't seen any activity, if you didn't look through the DIDSON or the ships sonar (which showed the mass of jellyfish but without detail, almost as a transitional boundary.)

All seemed to be going well, and the captain had asked me to come back to the bridge for a celebratory drink. It was about then that we realized that we had traveled to where we had originally been out of the main Cubosa area, but yet we were still surrounded.

They were following us.

What was worse, we were running out of ballast water. Thinking we were escaping, we were instead becoming more surrounded. It would be over in less than a couple hours.

Just before dawn, dejected, I went back to the bridge. The captain was meeting with some of the scientists. A few early risers were attempting to grasp the situation. I could tell right away, they were not buying the story. The sea was calm now. There was no sign of aggression from the Cubosa. The scientists (three of them) began openly mocking the captain and then me when I tried to explain things. I thought:

Well, we're going to run out of ballast water within the next hour, from what the captain had told me. So, it will almost be worth dying to see the smiles wiped off the faces of those scientists when they saw the first wave of Cubosa hit… and it would be in broad daylight too.

At 6:30 am, we could see the first hint of dawn, it was at that time the ballast tanks finally showed empty. We, or at least those of us who'd endured the worst—except Jonah who was in the infirmary—stood together solemnly looking out over the now calm water, awaiting the next and perhaps the last attack.

"That's weird," someone said, behind us. It was the watch captain. He had been monitoring the regular ship's regular sonar. "It looks like a layer of the sea is dropping away."

The captain, without turning away from the window said, "Old trick of the sonar, first noticed in WWII. It's all the plankton and such, sinking. They come up at night and sink during the day."

"And the jellyfish follow." I practically yelled out. Then I bolted for the door and ran to the winch deck lab. I called the captain and asked if he was sure that the ballast water had run out because I wasn't seeing any Cubosa near the ship. Of course, it was pointing nearly straight up but it was confirming what the sonar said.

"Probably take a while for the salinity to return, even after the last of the ballast," the captain said.

"Yeah," I said. "Probably right."

But we waited and waited, and by nine A.M. we were pretty sure we were in the clear. A million years of conditioning, the ancient diurnal cycle of rising and lowering with the sun had trumped intelligence. I started to laugh, sitting there in that stupid shipping container lab. It seemed so simple. Yet, as though having my life flash before my eyes, I relived every example from my own life where simple and ancient biological urges—urges I share with the most basic of God's creation—have triumphed over my own enlightened self-interest.

To complete the tale, Jonah was not okay. We sailed to a coordinate, close enough to be within chopper range and he was airlifted to a hospital. It was close but I understand he's doing alright now. I wish I could have gotten him up that ladder sooner, but at least he did better than his namesake.

I am still working at AIMS; I compartmentalize well. Thankfully, they don't take offense at my sideline. I'm doing groundbreaking work, using the DIDSON offshore to predict dangerous situations on beaches and in recreational underwater areas.

Somewhere out there in the Great Western Gyre, most likely within a smaller area (merely the size of Texas), is an organism—a single rudimentary brain perhaps the size of a large city—an organism with a billion eyes, and uncountable venomous barbs, visiting our beaches and returning with food and perhaps observations. It isn't a creature new to our world but it is, in effect, gaining cells at a rate it has never been able to do before. The conditions are perfect. We've practically knocked out its only regulator, the sea turtle, and we created warming and more acidic oceans which favor

Cubosa. One day perhaps it will, if it has not already, gain self-awareness.

One final note: When Menken and I reviewed the tapes we made of the electrical signals—the Mega-Cubosa EEG, if you will. We came to a disturbing conclusion when we compared our human states of consciousness at different brainwave rates, to the Cubosa creature. At one cycle per second, we are alive but unconscious. At a little higher frequency and we're dreaming. At five to seven, we're in a drowsy, almost hypnagogic state, a state where if disturbed we might mumble, wave an arm at our tormentor and just try to pull the covers back over our heads. It was at that frequency that the Cubosa was operating when the ship disturbed it. Like a creature half-asleep, it wasn't striking out with any real purpose or control. One day, I fear, it may grow large enough—have enough nodes—to become fully awake. What will it then become and, most importantly, what will we be to it?

Made in the USA
Charleston, SC
15 March 2013